SCULPT YOURSELF

SCULPT YOURSELF

SAVY

Sculpt Yourself

ISBN: 978-1-7324643-3-9

Cover Design by Savy Leiser
Edited by Lauri Dietz with Sarah Tierney
Formatted by Chelsea Lauren

For Sarah and Aimee*, who spent all of college watching weird sitcoms, reality shows, and teen dramas with me. Thank you for always encouraging me to be my weird self, and for being your weird selves too. Let's never stop making cool stuff together.*

ALSO BY SAVY

The Making of a Small-Town Beauty King

Furever Home Friends Series

Princess Allee

Smile, Chewie

Just Me, Wrigley

Kringle's Christmas

1

AMBER

I hate marketing. I hate the way commercials, billboards, social media campaigns, whatever, make their profit by emotionally manipulating people.

"It's just *capitalism*, Amber," Judie always says. Judie likes using big words here and there to sound smart because she doesn't realize that almost everything she says is stupid.

Okay, maybe that's not fair. Judie's my little sister, and I love her—how could I not, after she supported me through everything with our mom? And after she's given me so many free double-shot espresso drinks as part of *her* employee discount at Big Mama's Coffee—but sometimes the things she says just make no goddamn sense.

Like all the times in high school, when she'd try to get me to paint my nails with her, and I'd have to say, "Sorry, Judie. I can't paint my nails because I bite them obsessively, and I don't want to eat all that ammonia."

She'd say, "That's nail polish *remover* that has ammonia. And you should really stop biting your nails." Then she'd pull my hand away from my mouth (because, more often than not, I was already halfway to biting my nails again when she said this). "It's unsanitary. And they'd look much better if you didn't keep them so short."

This argument continued through high school, college, and beyond. It always ended with me rolling my eyes, and saying something like, "I'm a lesbian, Judie."

And then Judie would say something like, "What does that have to do with your nails?"

And then I'd roll my eyes again, so hard I occasionally worried they'd get lost in the back of my head. Because if by age twenty-two Judie hadn't figured out why lesbians might want to have short nails, she probably never would.

Anyway, I don't hate Judie. I like her enough to share an apartment with her, even two years after graduating from college. After *I* graduated, I mean. Judie didn't go to college. She's perfectly content working the rest of her life away at Big Mama's Coffee. I wonder what it's like to have so little ambition. I imagine it must be nice since it means she likes her current job enough to want to stay there forever.

Big Mama's Coffee doesn't advertise. That's another reason I like them. They just have a Twitter account and a Yelp page and a flashy sign out front. No loud commercials to bombard me in the face while I'm just trying to smoke a bowl and watch some *Everybody Loves Raymond* and *Friends* reruns.

Watching sitcoms isn't quite the same since Brianne moved away. Brianne was my roommate and best friend in college. We used to have Sitcom Night, where we'd watch all those stereotypical sitcoms from the 90s and 2000s—the kind where the bumbling husband ends up with a wife who's way too pretty for him, and manages to put up with all his bullshit because he's the breadwinner. Because men always make a solid household income even with no brains to speak of, and women are always gorgeous gold-diggers, right?

Brianne and I would take a shot every time someone made a joke that relied on gender stereotypes. We'd usually pass out before the end of two episodes.

If we didn't pass out, we'd make a new rule: chug an entire glass of whatever we've been drinking, if in all the episodes we watched, two characters of different races never interacted with each other. Which was almost every episode of every show we watched. So we'd always end up chugging an entire glass of something hard, usually rum, and then fall asleep mumbling about how unrealistic sitcoms are.

"You know because we're both women, and we're going into STEM fields, and you're gay as hell, Amber, so you'll never end up with a bumbling husband, and I'm black and you're white, and *we're* interacting," Brianne would slur, then pass out with her head against my shoulder.

But then we graduated from West Loop College, and Brianne got a job offer doing software development at this tiny little company in Des Moines, Iowa, so she moved out of Chicago, and now we mostly text.

And I *guess* we "both went into STEM fields," since I do tech support.

I guess, if you squint hard enough, reminding old people that copy-and-paste is a thing could be STEM.

Now I watch sitcoms with Judie.

Sometimes it's fun because she has a similar sense of humor as me, and we both enjoy stuffing our faces while watching TV. But sometimes it's less fun because if I ever want to smoke while we watch, Judie always groans and says, "You're a pot head."

"I get high, like, once a week. I'm not a pot head," I always say.

"You shouldn't do *any* drugs. They're bad for you."

"You work in a coffee shop. Caffeine is a drug."

Judie always shakes her head at that. "No it's not."

Like I said, a lot of the things Judie says are stupid.

Anyway, I hate marketing. I hate this dumb-ass commercial that's playing on the TV in Judie's and my living room right now. It's for these new soy potato chips. (So I guess they're not really potato chips at all. Just soy chips.)

All these people on TV munching on the soy chips are skinny white yuppies. Middle-aged soccer moms who giggle and say things like, "Ooooh, I'm being *bad*," when all they're doing is eating some goddamn ice cream or splurging on full-price yogurt or something, not snorting coke off of hookers.

But it's okay to be "bad," the soy chip commercial tells me. It reminds me in bright-orange block letters that these chips are...wait for it...*guilt-free*!

Because I guess eating is supposed to naturally come with guilt? That's what this commercial is implying.

If eating induced guilt by default, I'd spend my entire life in a state of constant remorse. Regular, run-of-the-mill, non-soy, full-fat potato chips constitute probably 30% of my diet. Well, along with off-brand cheese curls and tangy southern barbecue sauces.

I'm still skinnier than most of the soy-chip yuppies on TV.

I'm what all the cute girls back in high school would non-affectionately refer to as "a stick." Meaning that, not only am I blessed with a low body-fat percentage, but I am also cursed with a notable lack of tits and ass, all of which I tend to hide under one of my baggy zip-up hoodies.

When we were growing up, my parents—and Judie, to an extent—would worry that I had a tapeworm or something. Because how does a kid stuff herself with junk all day, and stay thin as a rail?

Well, as a kid, it was because I played a lot of sports. But I'm a lazy adult. I stay skinny because I eat *only* junk food. Most people get fat because they eat three meals a day, plus cake or whatever. I'd just eat cake instead of a meal. So it's fewer calories in total. Don't worry, I'm under no misconception that I'm healthy. I'm just too lazy to cook real food.

All through my life, it was *marketing*—it was *commercials* and *advertisements*—that told me my body wasn't desirable to men. Hell, it was marketing that told me men's opinions mattered in the first place. I think that's what first caused my distrust in marketing: the fact that I've never been attracted to a man in my life.

So I guess it's a good thing marketing doesn't apply to me.

It applies to Judie, though. Judie is *very* attracted to men. She's had a few boyfriends (all of whose names I've since forgotten) that have only lasted for a few weeks each.

But it's not just that. Judie also seems to hate her body, and seems weirdly jealous of mine.

I try to remind her that I'm just as flat-chested as she is, but the truth is, she's about twice my size everywhere else. Judie carries a lot of fat in her stomach and her face, which she hates. I'm not sure why it's such a big deal. I probably wouldn't even notice if she didn't bring it up every ten minutes.

She's always saying things like, "I don't even *mind* that I weigh this much. I just wish the fat could collect in my boobs and my butt rather than my face and my stomach."

I usually just shrug at that. Because what is there even to say to something like that?

I sure as hell can't agree with her, or she'll bite my head off. And I can't disagree, or else I'll get in an argument. And I really don't want to spend my time outside of work getting into petty arguments with my sister about her body fat composition.

I'd rather just shove more non-soy potato chips in my face, and wait for today's rerun of *Friends* to come back on so that Judie will start laughing at Phoebe and stop chastising me for having a joint on my Saturday afternoon.

But before we return to *Friends*, we have to sit through one more annoying commercial.

This one starts off by dramatically fading the whole screen to black. Then, punctuated with the loud *thump* of a bass drum, bright-red words appear on the screen: SCULPT YOURSELF.

2

KELLY

I LOVE MARKETING. IT'S A FUN WAY TO MIX THE corporate with the creative.

In college, I was a marketing major. I'm aware that that's the most cliché thing I could do as a millennial. But I minored in art, so at least I felt like I still got to follow my passion, especially now that I get paid to use my knowledge of color theory and visual composition every day.

I work in the Visual Marketing department at Finnegan & Peters. We're a mid-sized advertising firm located in downtown Chicago.

Wow, I sound like such a yuppie right now.

It's Monday afternoon, and I'm starting to feel what some of the managers call "the 3pm slump."

Rebecca, who sits at the desk next to mine, calls it the "7th inning stretch," then stands up and does some yoga poses by her desk. Sometimes she wears her plastic Harry Caray glasses when she does them. Rebecca is a goof. But she's also the main person who helped me feel welcome in Chicago when I moved here two years ago. She took me to Cubs games, she showed me around Millennium Park, and she made me feel at home for the first time since I left upstate New York.

So the 3pm slump: basically, I have two hours left in the work day, and I need some more coffee.

I've had two cups already today, and going for a third makes me feel kind of weak, if I'm being totally honest.

But if I'm being totally, *completely* honest, I just feel weak because last week was Health Week at Finnegan & Peters, where they gave us all gym membership vouchers and hosted panels of health experts each day during our lunch break. They'd talk to us about the importance of getting eight hours of sleep a night, cutting back on caffeine, and watching our sugar intake.

Our CEO, Bob Finnegan, and our COO, Melissa Peters, like to pretend it's because they care about the wellbeing of all their employees and want to create a healthy, lively work environment.

But we all know it's because they're paying for our health insurance, and can't afford for the premiums to go up. So better make sure we're all healthy.

Things like Health Week remind me that running a mid-sized advertising firm is just a lot of logistics and carefully calculated decisions. Still, I'd like to have my own business one day. Maybe I'll find a way to make logistics fun.

So I get my third coffee from our office coffee machine near the front entrance, place my coffee down on my desk, and head to the bathroom for a short break.

Usually, I like to use the bathroom downstairs. That one's usually not as crowded because it's the one we share with the bottom floor of our next-door-neighbor office suite, Costello's Accounting Firm. They just have their small tech support department (which I think is, like, two people) in their basement, so I can almost always get that bathroom to myself.

But it's 3pm, and I have more than two hours of work left to finish, so I use this floor's hallway bathroom instead. If I went downstairs, I might be tempted to fall asleep on the toilet, and there's a good chance no one would find me until a janitor knocked on the door at 8pm. (That only happened once. I missed the express Purple Line around the Loop, so I had to take the Brown Line, which goes around the Loop the opposite way. Getting home took forever.)

Washing my hands, I check my hair in the bathroom mirror. I added these electric blue streaks into my hair this past weekend. At first, I wasn't sure if I could do that in a corporate environment, but then Rebecca came in last week with her hair dyed red and blue for the Cubs, and I realized it was okay (as long as the dye is temporary, Rebecca told me the HR department told her). So now I've got my dark-brown, almost black, hair reaching slightly past my shoulders, with a pretty blue stripe framing my face on each side.

My bangs are getting kinda long. They're starting to dust the top of my brown tortoiseshell glasses, and I'm wondering if I need a haircut soon. Or if I should put a blue stripe in my bangs as well. I guess it couldn't hurt since the dye is temporary.

I subtly adjust my bra a little—boobs seem to be in the

right place, so that's good—and finish wiping my hands off on my jeans before returning to my desk.

When I slide back into my seat, Rebecca's still in downward dog pose. Her head's upside down, and I notice that the red-and-blue streaks are starting to fade out of her hair, leaving it mostly chestnut brown.

"I'm thinking of starting a book club," Rebecca says, holding completely still in her yoga pose. The Harry Caray glasses are sitting on her desk. I think she realized that they tend to fall off when she does downward dog.

I slide my chair in toward my computer and take a sip of my coffee. "That sounds fun. Like one for our office?"

Rebecca collapses down into child's pose. "Nope," she says, her voice muffled by the fact that her head's tucked into her knees. "We already have too many Finnegan & Peters groups. Finnegan & Peters softball team. Finnegan & Peters motherhood group. I want to make more friends outside our office."

"You always struck me as someone who has friends in every corner of the galaxy."

"True," Rebecca says, standing up. "But not enough in this office building."

"So, would it be, like, a building-wide book club?" I ask.

Rebecca shrugs. "Yeah, probably. You wanna join?"

"Yeah, sure. I really should read more."

That's what everyone says after college. *I should read more.* The only reason most people read in college was to pass their classes, and in most cases (mine included), we learned what we did and didn't need to read in order to do well on each assignment. I guess school sucks the joy of reading right out. 'Cause before high school, I used to read all the time. I even wrote a little *Harry Potter* fan-fiction here and there.

"Cool. I'll text you later when I figure out the details." Rebecca's now back in her chair. She smooths down the hair that got ruffled when she was upside down.

I down my third cup of coffee in four gulps and finally turn my attention back to the work on my computer screen. It's been calling my name for a while now.

Once I get back into the rhythm of working, it hits me. Shit. I have to pee again. I'm going downstairs to the good bathroom for this one.

3

AMBER

It's another Monday in the basement of Costello's Accounting Firm, and I feel like shit. I think I did too many shots with Judie last night. Judie didn't have to be at Big Mama's until noon today, and I've been here since 8am, so I'm stupidly jealous of her right now. At least since I'm the only one here right now, I can blast my YouTube playlist from my computer.

To cure my hangover, I've been slowly sipping the 64-ounce lemon-lime Gatorade I bought from the vending machine outside our office suite this morning.

"Office suite." I guess you could call it that. Don't get me wrong, Costello's Accounting Firm as a whole is definitely an office suite. But the basement room is just me and an outdated Windows desktop computer sitting on a beige formica desk. And a landline phone. That's so when the old people who work for Vivian Costello upstairs suddenly forget how to send emails, they can call me and ask me to come fix the internet.

Vivian Costello. Damn. I'm glad I don't have to work with her directly, or I'd never get anything done. (Don't get me wrong—I already don't get anything done. Fixing the internet is easier than it sounds, and people think you're magic for it.)

I'm not sure if I'd call Vivian Costello beautifully intimidating or intimidatingly beautiful. Before I met Vivian Costello, I had no idea middle-aged people could be sexy. Hell, I had no idea *taxes* could be sexy—or anything other than painfully boring, really.

I don't see Vivian Costello most days, but when I do, she's always wearing a different suit. She must have an entire closet full of suits. Some with pants, some with skirts, some with shoulder pads. All perfectly tailored to her body.

And when I'm on the main floor, lying under some old guy's desk, trying to restart his computer from the tower so his Microsoft Excel program will unfreeze, sometimes I'll hear Vivian Costello yell at Isabelle, the cute college intern, for giving her the wrong coffee or something. Vivian Costello means business. She's got this big, full, intimidating voice, decorated with her slight Italian accent. Sometimes when I hear it, I get chills, and I forget what I was doing under some old guy's desk in the first place.

For the first month I worked at Costello's Accounting, I was terrified of Vivian Costello. The second month, during my weekends, I often found myself lying on my bed, balancing my laptop on my stomach, and clearing all the embarrassing "lesbian accountant porn" Google searches from my browser history. (It's a thing that exists. I was surprised, too. Pleasantly surprised.)

Maybe I'm weird. I don't know. Judie has a crush on her

boss, too, so it can't be that unusual. Her boss, the manager of Big Mama's Coffee, is a giant teddy bear of a guy named Luke. (I think his actual mom might be the Big Mama. I wonder how she feels about that name. Maybe she picked it.) Though, unlike the scary, forty-five-year-old Vivian Costello, Luke is a twenty-eight-year-old goofball. So maybe it's actually kind of different.

So I'm spinning in my foamy black desk chair, sipping the last of my Gatorade, and thinking about all this, when something snaps me out of my trance.

My playlist on YouTube has stopped for another ad. And it's not just any stupid ad that reminds me why I hate marketing, but it's THE stupid ad. The awful SCULPT YOURSELF ad I saw with Judie this past Saturday.

It's this dramatic-ass black-and-white ad, with this conventionally beautiful, blonde European lady standing against a white background, wearing a black bikini. I mean, it's black-and-white other than her blood-red lipstick, which is popping on-screen. She's illuminated in chiaroscuro lighting, giving the ad a film-noir quality, and the background music is this slow, romantic tenor saxophone solo. It's very sexual, but not in a way that would actually turn anyone on. In more of a disturbing way. She starts off by grabbing lumps of fat on her thighs and slowly moving them up to her breasts, all the while swaying sensually with the music. I don't think she opens her eyes even once. Then, when she's done, she keeps swaying, but now she's got this perfect hourglass figure. Then the screen goes black again, and it says "SCULPT YOUR-

SELF WITH LIPAMORPH" in bright-red cursive letters.

I feel like I'm in the Twilight Zone or something.

Then, I think, I'm kinda bored, and no one's been calling me to fix their internet or remind them how to send an email, so maybe I'll actually watch a few episodes of *The Twilight Zone* to pass the time.

But then, all 64 ounces of Gatorade catch up with me, and I realize I *really* have to pee.

So I get up, and go to the little hallway bathroom outside our "office suite." I like this bathroom because it has three stalls, but it's usually empty. Meaning that no one will judge me if I fall asleep on the toilet. (I haven't yet, but it's bound to happen one of these days. And then everyone's internet will remain broken forever.)

So I'm in the middle stall, texting Brianne and aggressively peeing out the entire bottle of Gatorade, when I realize that, for the first time since I started working here, I'm not the only one in this bathroom.

"Can you pass me some toilet paper?" the other person in here asks, sticking a hand under the stall door.

I take a second longer than normal to respond since I'm a little surprised that there's another person in here. "Yeah, sure."

"I don't think they restock the toilet paper that often since no one ever uses this bathroom," she laughs.

I bunch up a ball of toilet paper and look down for her hand. Before I pass the ball of toilet paper to her, I stare at her hand for a second. She's got short nails like mine, but it's clear from how smooth they are that she cuts them, instead of biting like me. She also has four of her nails painted a dark forest green, with her ring fingernail painted a metallic silver.

It's pretty.

I hand her the toilet paper. Then I finish my text to Brianne about the weird SCULPT YOURSELF commercial, and how if she were here, we'd make a drinking game to it.

This bathroom has two sinks, with only one soap dispenser between them. So when we're washing our hands after leaving the stalls, my hand briefly fights hers for access to the soap.

So I decide to just say it. "I like your nails."

She smiles at me, and that's when the fluorescent bathroom lights catch the electric blue streaks in her hair.

"And your hair," I add, almost throwing my hand over my mouth. (I don't, but my hand does twitch a little.) I need to shut up before this girl thinks I'm in love with her or something. But then I remember that girls give each other compliments all the time, so I can chill. Maybe. *Can* I chill?

"Thanks," she laughs. "I like your freckles."

Wow. If I've ever been envious of someone's confidence, it's right now. Like, here I am freaking out over telling this girl that her hair and nails are pretty, which is a totally normal thing to say, and she just tells me she likes my *freckles*, like it's no big deal. I mean, it's not a big deal, but, just, wow.

Then I remember that complimenting me really *isn't*

anything for her to freak out over because it's statistically most probable that she's straight, and this is just another friendly everyday interaction for her.

Then I realize that I actually don't know if she's straight, or any other thing about her because I literally just met this girl two minutes ago, and all we've done is share toilet paper, and I don't even know her name.

So I extend my hand to her and say, "Nice to meet you. I'm Amber Stiles, from tech support."

"I'm Kelly," she says, shaking my hand, "from Marketing."

4

JUDIE

Sometimes I help Big Mama's Coffee with their marketing. We're a small enough business that we don't have any marketing people on staff, which means we don't have any kind of designated social media manager. So sometimes I manage Big Mama's Twitter from my phone when we're having a slow day.

So far today, I've tweeted photos of nine different lattes I've made. I like to do that cool latte art, where you draw pictures with the foam. Right now, I'm finishing up a pumpkin spice latte (it's early September, so we're having to make a lot of those lately) in a pretty green ceramic mug for a lady named Greta who's sitting near the window. I quickly snap a photo before calling her name. It's not my best work. I tried to draw a pumpkin in the foam, but it came out looking kind of like an amoeba.

Just as I'm posting a new tweet from @bigmamacoffee, Amber bursts through the front door and flops down on one of our burgundy velvet couches.

"You made it out of the Loop fast. Espresso?"

Amber shrugs. She shrugs more than any person I know.

I'm not sure if it's because she's indecisive or apathetic. "Not feeling caffeine right now. How about a black tea?"

"Black tea also has caffeine."

Again, the shrug. "That's fine. Just dilute it with cream or something." She eyes the baked goods under the glass panel to my right. "And a muffin."

"My employee discount doesn't work on muffins. Especially for other people."

Amber doesn't answer. She just slides down on the couch.

"Bad day?"

Again with the shrugs.

"I'm gonna make a new drinking game. We take a shot every time you shrug."

Amber chuckles to herself. "All right, fair enough. No, it wasn't a particularly bad day. Just boring. And I was a little hungover."

Behind the counter, I start brewing her black tea.

"And...never mind."

"What?" I don't look up from the clean white mug I'm filling with hot water. As the mug fills, the tea bag starts to float.

"Who's in charge of the music here?"

"Since it's just me for the afternoon shift today, I am."

"So why did you pick the world's most headache-inducing playlist?" Amber rubs her forehead. I think she sometimes forgets that you can take Ibuprofen for a hangover. (It's Tylenol you can't take.)

"Because I'm the only one working here, and I like it."

I've got Miz Lollipop's new album, *Bubblicious*, playing from my laptop, which I plugged into our speakers behind the counter. Amber showed me how to do that last year when I got this job since she likes to verify to herself that her tech support knowledge has a practical purpose. She regrets it every time I put one of my, as she would say, "basic" playlists on.

"This song sounds like a synthesizer got fucked up at an '80s coke party and had an illegitimate love child with a dying whale."

I roll my eyes and start pouring the cream into her tea. "You're so dramatic, Amber."

"I'm not dramatic. I'm witty."

Now it's my turn to chuckle.

The song currently playing is Miz Lollipop's "Worship Dat Booty," probably the biggest hit off her new album. I like to say this song is a feminist anthem about men learning to worship women and women learning to embrace their sexuality. Amber says this song objectifies women and reduces them to sex toys (I guess by worshipping their booties instead of their minds or something?).

But Amber also conveniently ignores the fact that Miz Lollipop is one of the few female rappers to make it big. (And, don't tell anyone, but Amber's all talk. I've caught her listening to Eminem in her room a few times when she's in a bad mood.)

I turn around to face her and set the hot mug of tea on the counter. "So, what were you going to tell me earlier?"

"What?" She gets the tea off the counter and sits back down on the couch.

"You were all like, 'Work was so stupid and boring and...never mind.' What was the *never mind*?"

"Judie, I'm not sure if anyone's told you this before, but when someone says *never mind*, it means they don't actually want to continue talking about that thing. For a social butterfly, you sure do miss a lot of cues."

I giggle quietly. There's *something* up her butt. And I'm gonna tease it out of her.

"Did pretty Miss Costello catch you staring?"

"I didn't even *see* her. We don't even work on the same floor. I was by myself all day. Until Samantha came in at 4:30, I mean."

"Oh." I giggle again. "So you're saying you spent all day jerking off to thoughts of her."

"Ew!" Amber chokes on her tea a little. (It's for show. I know she doesn't actually think that was gross.) "Fine, Judie. Have you ever..."

"Have I ever what?"

"Ugh. This is so stupid. Have you ever...told someone that you liked their *freckles*?"

"What?" As far as I know, I've never used that specific compliment on anyone. "No. I don't think so. I mean...maybe I'd tell Luke I like his freckles. If he had any. But he doesn't, so I don't."

"Okay. So what I'm getting from you is that if you tell someone you like their freckles, it's definitely flirting?"

I slam the counter with the palms of my hands so hard at

that moment that Greta by the Window looks up from her pumpkin spice latte and briefly pulls out one of her earbuds. (I forgot she was still in here until right now.) I drop my voice a bit. "Did Costello tell you she liked your freckles?"

"No! Like I said, I didn't even see her today. And Vivian Costello is not...it's not like..."

"She's not a real prospect. Just your spank bank. Got it."

Amber rolls her eyes at that too. I feel successful every time I make Amber roll her eyes, groan, or sigh. I guess it's part of my duty as her little sister. (Well, "little" as in, I'm two years younger. I probably weigh twice what she does. But neither of us wants to talk about that right now.)

"What I'm trying to say," Amber continues, "is that I met this girl today. And she told me she liked my freckles. And I don't know what to make of that."

"Was she cute?"

"Do we have to focus on her appearance?"

"Okay. So you're saying yes, she was cute."

Sometimes I feel kind of bad for Amber. It can't be easy trying to navigate all this all the time. I mean, it's not for me either—but like, she needs to second-guess all these basic interactions she has all the time. Back when we were in high school, I used to be kind of jealous of Amber. (Well because she was skinny, but that's another story.) Amber would never, *never once in her life*, need to worry about getting pregnant.

But then, at the end of my sophomore year (her senior year), she had this awful incident that involved taking this straight girl to prom, and I realized that she didn't have it so easy either. (And, for the record, that girl 100% led her on. But neither of us wants to talk about *that* right now, either.)

I notice Greta leaving the table by the window and exiting Big Mama's Coffee, so I come out from behind the counter and sit in the armchair across from Amber. "So, did you get her number?"

Amber shakes her head and sips her tea.

"What about her name?"

Amber sighs at that. "Her name...was Kelly from Marketing."

5

KELLY

I like your freckles?!

How did that even come out of my mouth?

My whole ride home on the Purple Line, I stare out the window and contemplate my life. Okay, maybe that is a bit dramatic. Still, I contemplate *something*.

I guess I contemplate Amber's freckles. And I contemplate why I sometimes have no filter and just let these super awkward things slip out of my mouth. And I contemplate who I should text for advice.

Zack?

Zack and I haven't talked really since I left New York, but we like to say we're still friends. We still like each other's Facebook statuses and stuff, so I guess that kinda counts.

I could ask Rebecca, I guess. But I'm not sure Rebecca gets it. Rebecca's been dating this guy named Quentin for the past six years, and they got engaged about a year ago. So I don't think Rebecca remembers what it's like feeling awkward when you meet someone attractive.

Also, I'm not sure if "awkward" is a word in Rebecca's

vocabulary. When Rebecca met Quentin, she probably just walked right up to him and said, "You're cute. Let's date." Yeah. I can definitely see Rebecca doing something like that.

When the train stops at Belmont, I get off and start walking home.

And I think about how I really don't need to second-guess every interaction I have with someone.

Once inside my apartment, I decide to chill and focus on my art for the rest of the night.

My favorite thing about working in marketing at Finnegan & Peters is that we all make pretty decent money. I guess that makes me, as an artist, kind of a corporate sell-out. But I don't really mind being a corporate sell-out because it means I can afford a 1200 square-foot apartment in Lakeview all by myself. (Well, along with my cat, Sienna. But Sienna doesn't pay rent.)

My favorite thing about my apartment is that, without a roommate, I can have an entire room as my art studio. My art studio has this giant wooden desk with legs made of PVC piping (Zack made it for me during his woodworking phase in college), a torn green armchair that I found near a dumpster (because there's nothing wrong with wanting to be comfortable while you make art, but you don't want to use a nice new chair that might get dirty), and then my supplies scattered around the room. I've got art samples thumbtacked all over the walls (I didn't ask the landlord before I did that, but for the amount I pay each month, I can do whatever the hell I want to these walls): mostly watercolor portraits of Sienna, some colored pencil still-lifes I did on printer paper, and the *Harry Potter* fan art I made as a teenager (yes, he's kissing Draco Malfoy in some of it).

I think the portraits of Sienna are my favorite. She's this gorgeous brown-red color (yes, she's technically burnt sienna; I thought I was so clever for that when I named her in college), and she's got these bright green-grey eyes that really pop in watercolor.

I only put hand-made art on my walls. I have to do enough graphic designing at work; I don't need to think about it at home.

I sit in my armchair with a mug of decaf tea and my sketchbook. I set the tea down on the wooden desk to my left and open my sketchbook up on my lap.

Sometimes I want coffee in the evenings. I know I shouldn't since I had three cups at work today and I don't want to be up all night, but the smell of coffee goes well with drawing. Maybe that's just because, sophomore year of college, I did this whole series of art called "Doodles in Coffee Stains on Napkins."

There's this coffee shop a few blocks from me called Big Mama's. I make a mental note to give it a try one of these days.

Then I flip to my current page in the sketchbook: anatomy studies.

I've always been pretty good at drawing people. Not to be arrogant, or anything. I just like the way I draw them. The body always fascinates me. Like, you can learn the proportions of the face and the standard composition of a body, but there are *so* many intricacies. I feel like I could study this forever.

Because in some ways, everyone's body is exactly the same. The centers of our eyes line up with the corners of our mouths. Things like that. But our bodies are also so, *so* different. And it amazes me how many small differences we can notice among ourselves, if we analyze ourselves for long enough.

So that's why I'm still doing anatomy studies.

I've got a stash of *Playboy* magazines under my armchair. I don't know why I hide them there. I'm not a teenage boy in the '90s. They're for art purposes, and it's not like Sienna's gonna judge me or something.

Don't get me wrong; I didn't *pay* for them. I'd never financially support such a sexist publication. I stole them from my dad's bottom desk drawer before I left for college.

(Maybe I am a teenage boy.)

I like drawing from *Playboys* because even though the ladies in them all have the "ideal" body type, they're still all so different. Some have these giant boobs but no hips, and some have these perfectly pear-shaped bodies with these super thick thighs, while still maintaining flat stomachs.

I used to wonder how they did it. How they got bodies that well-proportioned. I don't have to wonder anymore since we all know now. How *some* of them did it, at least. I know some of them just worked out a lot.

I start on today's sketch: Jessica from page 14.

I'm also not sure when I realized my interest in the female body went beyond academic curiosity. Beyond "art purposes."

And I'm also not sure when I realize that Jessica from page 14 is covered in pretty brown freckles.

6

AMBER

Judie and I are watching *How I Met Your Mother* and taking a sip of rum every time it's the exact same show as *Friends*.

Sometimes we disagree on when to drink. "There's no Phoebe character!" Judie protests. "So it can't be *that* similar!"

"Why do you care?" I ask. "You're a Rachel anyway."

That's when that stupid SCULPT YOURSELF commercial comes back on.

This one's worse. I mean, it's partially better because they got rid of that creepy-ass blonde lady and her creepy red lipstick, but it's also worse because they replaced her with Miz Lollipop.

On the one hand, I *want* to like Miz Lollipop because she's an awesome, empowered black woman, and her first album has this song on it about how she doesn't need a man to make money. So I was glad that message was going into the mainstream.

I actually considered going to one of her concerts with Judie after I heard this one song she did where she sampled

"Pretty Woman" in the background and did this rap on top of it where she gave a shoutout to all these women she admired and found attractive. It was very, *very* gay. And I was like, "Maybe Miz Lollipop is cool and progressive!"

But then I watched this interview with her on TV where they asked her about the "homoerotic subtext" in that song (which was stupid because trust me, there was no subtext; this song was *blatantly gay*), and she was all giggly, like, "Oh, it was totally unintentional. I didn't mean it in a gay way."

I hate that phrase. Reminds me of fucking Lindsey, from high school.

(Not like, *fucking Lindsey*. Like, "stupid Lindsey, dumb-ass Lindsey, annoying-bitch-that-I-never-want-to-see-again Lindsey." But I don't want to talk about Lindsey right now.)

And *then* this new album, *Bubblicious*, that Judie's been listening to nonstop, barely meets the basic definition of music.

Anyway, Miz Lollipop's on TV right now, with the vamp to "Worship Dat Booty" playing softly in the background behind her. (I only recognize the song because Judie plays it so much at Big Mama's.)

"Do you want to know how me and all my girls got this body?" she asks.

Not particularly, I think to myself, but I can tell that Judie's interested, so I keep watching.

On the screen, images of a few other mid-2010s celebrities appear. There's Betty J, who's really just the white version of Miz Lollipop—same basic straight-girl music, just this time coming out of a blonde. Though, I'd probably say Miz Lollipop is more talented because at least she can rap—and then there's Ella Esmeralda, who doesn't make music or act or anything. Actually, I think she's just famous for having a great ass. (Which, I won't lie, she does have.)

Miz Lollipop is thin everywhere except for her boobs, which are decently large, and her butt, which seems bigger than humanly possible. Like, it takes up the whole screen. Judie swears that the rumors about her having implants are false. I don't really care one way other the other, but Judie's very passionate about this topic, and it all comes out when she's drunk.

Then, Miz Lollipop goes on to introduce Lipamorph. "It's the only over-the-counter way to sculpt yourself," she says.

She then explains what it does, which is a lot more than that first commercial did. The first one just kind of showed that blonde lady moving her fat around like Play-Doh, and I guess was supposed to make you curious so you go to their website to find out more. But it just freaked me out, so I did not go to their website.

"Lipamorph loosens up all the fat cells in your body, so you can move them wherever you want. It's the way to get the body you've always wanted, for an affordable price."

The screen then goes on to show some before and after pictures. Betty J's in particular catches my eye. Her "before" picture shows almost the exact body type Judie has—small boobs, a round stomach, and a little extra fat in her cheeks, giving her a round face. The "after" picture shows her with a perfect hourglass figure. Giant DD-cup boobs, a tiny 26-inch waist, and a full, round butt, which descends into thick thighs and tapers out into smaller calves and ankles.

"It's what girls like Betty, Ella, and me have been using for years," says Miz Lollipop.

Well, I guess a lot of things make sense now. And, as Judie points out to me at least twice over the course of the commercial, she was *totally right* about Miz Lollipop not having implants.

But still, it's creepy as all hell.

I flop onto my back on our couch, realizing I'm a little tipsy from the rum. (*How I Met Your Mother* really is the exact same show as *Friends.*) "Yo, Judie, you want me to make some barbecue nachos?" I ask.

Judie's eyes are transfixed on the television screen in front of her. "No, you go on ahead," she says. "I'm gonna go to Walgreens."

"For what?"

Judie gestures to the screen. "I want to try that."

I sit straight up, forgetting that I'm mildly drunk. "Now wait just a minute. I thought you were against *drugs*, Judie?"

"I am," she says.

"Judie, I'm not sure if you're aware, but this Lipamorph is a drug."

Judie shakes her head. I think she's a tiny bit drunk, too. "No, Amber, it's a *medicine*. That's like saying Tylenol is a drug. Or birth control or chemo."

"Those are all examples of drugs."

Judie rolls her eyes at me. "You don't get to decide what a *drug* is, Amber. You're not the drug police."

"The drug police? Judie, drug crimes are handled by the regular police."

"I'm so done with you right now," Judie says, standing up. She stumbles a little (I guess she's more than a *tiny* bit drunk), then heads out the door, still wearing her black tank top and pink plaid pajama pants.

Well, I guess I have the apartment to myself for now. So, despite it being a Monday, I head to my room to get my glass pipe and do what is, indisputably, *drugs*.

7

JUDIE

After I get back from Walgreens, I head to my bedroom, where I strip down to just my bra and underwear.

I read the instructions on that thin piece of paper that comes in the Lipamorph box.

I have to take the pill. Then, once it takes effect, I have five minutes to shift my fat around. After five minutes, it will lock into place. Then, after a week, it will start to shift back to its original position, and I'll have to get another pill at the store.

Seems easy enough.

I stand in front of the full-length mirror on my closet door, holding the little pink pill in my hand. Well, here goes—

"Hold up, I wanna watch!"

A very drunk Amber kicks my door open, holding a plate of barbecue-sauce drenched nachos in one hand and cradling a giant plastic bowl of buttery popcorn under her opposite arm. She sets her snacks on the floor, then flops onto my pink velvet beanbag chair.

"Why do you want to watch?"

Amber shrugs and shoves a fistful of popcorn into her mouth. Even from a few feet away, I can smell the weed in her hair. That clears a few things up. "I guess I take a sort of dark, condescending form of amusement in it."

"You can be very self-aware when you're under the influence, Amber."

"I'm always self-aware," Amber mumbles through a mouthful of popcorn. Then she bites into a barbecue-sauce-covered chip.

"Not the first adjective I'd use to describe you."

"You're not the adjective police," she giggles, flopping onto her side. Amber is high as hell right now.

I slosh around some saliva on my tongue, then pop the pill in my mouth and swallow with a gulp.

Amber's now lying on her back, with her head hanging upside-down over the side of my beanbag chair. She picks up pieces of popcorn and throws them into her mouth. She misses about half the time, but luckily, Amber has never minded eating off the floor.

Suddenly, this weird tingly feeling takes over my whole body. It's subtle in some places, like my feet, which feel almost normal. But then, around my stomach, it's like this intense buzzing feeling. Like a cell phone vibrating combined with the pins and needles you feel before you go numb.

I guess that means it's working.

I clamp my right hand around a clump of fat at the front of my stomach, and I push it up to my boobs.

The fat kind of tickles when it's moving. Like it's fuzzy

on the inside or something. Which, logically, I know it isn't. But it's just a really funny feeling.

Amber's staring at the ceiling, presumably feeling funny feelings as well.

"My toes feel so good right now, Judie."

"Glad to hear it."

"Like, I feel like they're made of silk. And I'm rubbing them against each other, and it's *just so smooth*."

"You sound like you need to go to bed."

"Wait, no, lemme see your new body first!"

I turn away from my mirror to face Amber.

"*Damn*, Judie! You got a booty!" she laughs. "Judie with a booty!"

"You could've seen that without me turning around. But thanks."

"You don't look like *you*, though."

"Go to bed, Amber."

I turn back around and look at myself. I do look different. My new boobs are spilling out of my bra. I'll have to get a new one. My waist is thin. I'm a perfect hourglass. I finally feel comfortable calling myself *curvy*.

Honestly, I look hot as hell.

But I'll need to get used to the feeling of having my weight distributed differently. I guess I never really noticed which parts of my body weighed more than other parts since I was always just used to my body feeling that way.

So, when I take my first step forward, I'm a little shocked by how top-heavy I feel. It leads me to tripping over my own feet and falling face-first down on the floor.

Amber bursts out laughing. I forgot she was still in here. Or aware enough of her surroundings to realize that just happened.

"Oh, Judie, I'm sorry," she says between laughs. "Are you okay?"

"Actually, yeah," I tell the floor. "These boobs are a pretty decent cushion."

8

AMBER

It's Tuesday in the basement of Costello's, and despite my gross hangover, I feel significantly better than I did yesterday. That's mostly because on Tuesdays Samantha works the morning shift along with me, so I have to do even less work than usual.

See, Samantha is actually *interested* in doing this. I think she majored in something computer-related, and now she's in between jobs while waiting to get something in programming.

I majored in Social Policy, with a Computer Science minor as a fallback. Turns out it's really, *really* hard to find jobs in social policy. So sometimes I write blog posts for *The Feminist Forum*, this online site that pays me $25 per article, but that's it.

So, anyway, Samantha's perfectly happy to take all the calls that come in from upstairs, which is like one every two hours or something ridiculous like that. I mean, it's ridiculous how often old people forget how to use the internet. But it's also ridiculous how little work we have to do.

While Samantha does all the work, I blast my Janis

Joplin playlist on YouTube and drink my coffee and Gatorade.

Separately, I mean. I've got a mug of coffee to my right and a bottle of Gatorade to my left. I don't mix coffee with Gatorade, but I *would* mix both of them with vodka. Not at work, though.

I take a sip of my coffee and let my mind wander.

Which, of course, leads it right back to Kelly from Marketing.

Kelly from Marketing has a cute smile. *Oh, God. I'm turning into a softy.* She works in *marketing,* I remind myself. Also, she's probably straight. I'm using "probably" in the purely statistical sense, of course.

Then why did she tell you she liked your freckles? While giving you the aforementioned cute smile?

Fuck. I hate this. Again, it reminds me of *fucking Lindsey.* And I can't even lie and say I don't want to think about Lindsey right now because I have literally nothing else to do at work.

Don't get me wrong, I have *no* feelings for Lindsey. Except bitterness, if that counts as an emotion. I haven't even seen her in six years.

Lindsey was my senior prom date.

Judie was a sophomore at the time, but a senior guy asked her to go with him, so she was getting to go. And I thought maybe it would be fun for me and Judie to hang out at prom together. You know, get some sister prom pictures. I don't know. It sounded cute in my head at the time.

But I didn't really want to go to prom alone, so I thought

maybe I could find a date. Most of my super close friends were already in relationships.

Also, one guy actually asked me. I told him to fuck off.

I know that's rude, and in retrospect, I actually feel really bad about it. See, pretty much everyone knew I was gay by senior year. I didn't keep it a secret. And I got plenty of shit for it (high school sucks), so I thought this guy was asking me sarcastically as a way of making fun of me.

It turned out that he was like the one guy in the universe who didn't know I wasn't into dudes, and he actually liked me.

So I feel like shit about that. But in my defense, I didn't actually know his intentions. Fucking Lindsey had no such excuse.

Lindsey and I were friends, but not like *best* friends. We were just in the same overall friend group because we both worked on the tech crew for school plays, so we hung out at cast parties and stuff.

I didn't have any friends that were gay in high school. Or, I might have, but no one was as confident as me to admit that as a teenager.

But Lindsey wasn't explicitly *not gay* either. I'd never seen her date a guy or even express any interest in any guy. And she was always talking about Beyoncé and how cool she thought Beyoncé was (which was reasonable because Beyoncé is cool as hell) and how much she loved Beyoncé's body and how she had the biggest crush on Beyoncé. These were all *her* words.

So Lindsey and I would hang out at play practice and

listen to Beyoncé together. And Lindsey seemed really interested in me. She'd be like, "Amber, you look really cute today!" and stuff like that, which had to be flirting because, trust me, I looked "cute" by almost *no* teenage girl's standards.

Two weeks before prom, I got the idea to ask Lindsey to go to prom with me. Seemed logical, yeah?

I even did one of those cool prom-posals that girls go so crazy over. It wasn't anything elaborate, but I thought it was cool. We were working on the lighting design for *A Midsummer Night's Dream* together, so I left her a note on the light board one day that said, "It would be my dream to spend a mid-spring night at prom with you."

Actually, in retrospect, it was super lame.

But it was *undeniably* a come-on. Like that one Miz Lollipop song, it was *explicitly gay*.

And Lindsey was like, "Yes, of course, I'd *love* to go to prom with you!"

I actually got really excited when she said yes. I think that was when I understood what people meant by your heart "skipping a beat."

Judie and I went prom dress shopping together. I think it was the most fun we ever had as sisters that didn't involve eating or watching crappy television. Judie and I had never gone shopping together before, or anything like that. But we helped each other pick out dresses that flattered our body types. I got this long red form-fitting dress. Even in high school, my wardrobe was 90% jeans and baggy hoodies, so this was way out of my element. But this prom was going to be *awesome*, I just knew it!

So Lindsey and I were slow-dancing together to "Time After Time." Pretty much your stereotypical prom scene. We were about the same height, so I think we alternated whose arms were around whose shoulders versus around their waist.

And, I guess, the mood just seemed right. Cyndi Lauper was singing her heart out, there were these little paper-lantern lights around us illuminating the school gym, and I was wearing a dress for only the second time in my life (the first was Communion when I was seven), so I went for it. I leaned in and kissed her.

At first, her mouth moved along a little, so I thought she was going along with it, and I remember thinking that she tasted a little bit like peach. But that all lasted about half a second, when she pulled her face away.

"What are you doing."

Not even as a question. Her voice punctuated that sentence with a period.

So I just said, "Sorry."

And she said, "No, it's okay, just...what?"

And I said, "Well, I figured since we're, like, prom dates..."

And she just said, "Yeah, but not in a gay way."

I think that's when I realized that straight girls are allowed to see the world a different way. (Don't even get me started on straight *guys*. I already knew they had it easy long ago. I didn't get a "Fuck the Patriarchy" tattoo under my left boob last year for nothing.)

Straight girls can go to prom with other girls, and it's assumed they're just friends. Straight girls can talk about their female celebrity crushes all day long, and everyone's just supposed to assume that they don't mean it in a gay way. Lindsey just wanted Beyoncé's aesthetic, or she was jealous of her dance moves or something. Nothing's ever meant in a gay way.

So Lindsey and I just kind of awkwardly walked away from each other. And Judie hung out with me all night while I cried in the bathroom. We were not the only ones.

I guess I *did* get the full prom experience, after all.

Last I saw on Facebook, Lindsey's engaged to some hipster guy with a beard so thick you could hide a flask in it. And I'm twenty-four years old, still bitterly daydreaming about prom at work. Fucking Lindsey.

I GET SNAPPED out of my trance when I hear the landline phone ringing. I crane my neck to look at Samantha's desk, but she's gone. She's probably solving a problem for one of the other calls I ignored.

Some guy upstairs can't figure out how to transfer files from his computer to a flash drive. He's apparently never heard the phrase *drag and drop* before. It's not even like, "I tried drag and drop and it didn't work!" No. He literally says to me, "What does drag and drop mean?"

I pause my YouTube playlist and head out to the hallway staircase that leads to the main floor of Costello's.

In the staircase, I run into this girl with faded red-and-blue stripes in her hair and these giant dangly Cubs earrings on. "Hey! I'm Rebecca!" she says.

Until I met Kelly from Marketing in the bathroom yesterday, I never realized our building was so friendly. Samantha barely says hi.

"I'm Amber."

"I'm trying to make more friends in this building," she says. "Do you want to join a book club?"

"That depends. Is it actually a book club or a pyramid scheme in disguise?"

Rebecca bursts out laughing. If only I could've been that smooth and witty with Kelly in the bathroom yesterday. *Statistically, Kelly's probably straight*, I remind myself.

That's when Kelly from Marketing bursts into the staircase. "Rebecca!" she calls. "There you are. I've been looking all over the office for you. I need you to forward me that email from John."

"Okay. But first, I'm trying to get Amber here to join our book club."

"Oh, hey," Kelly says, smiling at me. "You should join."

So I figure, hey, why not? I really *should* read more.

9

KELLY

Our first book club meeting is Friday at noon since most offices in the building take a lunch around then.

Rebecca did a fantastic job of making friends with most of the building. I'm shocked at how many people I don't know at our first meeting.

We hold the meetings in the basement room of Costello's. Amber offered it up since there's nothing ever happening in there except her and Samantha waiting for a call about how someone forgot how to copy and paste again.

So we're all sitting on the floor in a circle introducing ourselves.

"I'm Rebecca! You all know me already because I probably creepily approached you and pressured you into joining," she says with an unwavering smile.

Everyone nods.

"Anyway, I work in Visual Marketing at Finnegan & Peters." She gestures to me.

"Hi, I'm Kelly. I also work in Visual Marketing at Finnegan & Peters."

"I'm Isabelle. I'm an intern at Costello's Accounting."

"I'm Amber. I do tech support at Costello's."

"Samantha. I do tech support at Costello's too."

"I'm Fanny Spitzer. I'm the receptionist at Harmon, Jackson, & Harmon Law on the fifteenth floor."

"Why not Harmon, Harmon & Jackson?" Rebecca asks.

"I didn't name the law firm, sweetie."

Fanny Spitzer is at least in her forties, and she looks like one of those mom-types who would call anyone younger than her "sweetie." I can't tell if she means it in an endearing or condescending way. Rebecca doesn't appear to care.

"I'm Tanya. I'm a paralegal at Harmon, Jackson, & Harmon."

Finally, the last lady. Slumped in her chair, with her graying, frizzy brown hair, and her black leather jacket, she looks oddly familiar. "I'm Midge," she says, in a voice that screams *chain smoker*. "I'm one of the janitors for the whole building."

Oh.

She looks right at me. Shit. "Aren't you the girl that fell asleep on the toilet?"

I let out a nervous laugh. "Yep."

Amber bursts out laughing, and I feel my whole face heat up. "Oh man," she says. "I fantasize about doing that all the time!"

I start laughing along with her. "It's not that great, I promise."

Midge starts laughing too, and Fanny Spitzer looks at us like we've all lost our minds.

"So, let's pick out our first book," says Rebecca. She

crosses her legs on the floor in front of her and rolls up the sleeves of her thick Chicago Bears sweater. (I don't think Rebecca understands the first half of the phrase "business casual.")

She pulls a folded-up piece of yellow paper out of the back pocket of her jeans and scans the list of books she's written. "Well, my top choice is *Never Die Easy*," she says after a moment. "It's the biography of the legendary Walter Payton."

I *think* I know who Walter Payton is, but I don't want to ask because I'm worried Rebecca will yell at me to go back to New York. (In a friendly way, of course.)

Like, for example, once we were at a Cubs game together (my first one—it was like a week after I moved here and Rebecca started fully immersing me), and we were in line for beer, and I ordered a 312 from the Goose Island cart. But I said it like, "Can I have a three-twelve?"

And Rebecca just slapped my back really hard—she'd already had a few three-one-twos, as I've learned it's pronounced—and yelled right in my ear, "You want some flimsy folded-up pizza with that three-twelve, you New York trash?!"

So instead I just say, "Yeah, that sounds good. I was also thinking, what if we revisited novels from our childhood, like a nostalgic kind of thing? Like *Harry Potter* and stuff?"

Fanny Spitzer looks at me like I have three heads. "I was twenty-three when Harry Potter came out," she says, and I realize that we have at least two people in this group over the age of forty, so the nostalgic appeal might not work.

"I wasn't born yet when *Harry Potter* first came out," Isabelle squeaks.

I'm not exaggerating. *She squeaks*. This girl is adorable. But, not like in a sexual way. Like a puppy or something.

"This is *so cool*," Rebecca shouts, throwing her head back. "I love how this club is so multi-generational!" I'd be hard-pressed to find something Rebecca *doesn't* love. Flimsy, folded pizza, I assume.

So we all spend the rest of the lunch break talking about random stuff like that. We never decide on a book.

At one point, a Miz Lollipop song pops up in the YouTube playlist Amber's had on, and she rushes over to change it, mumbling about how her sister must've stuck it in there to troll her.

That ignites something in Fanny Spitzer. Apparently, she *hates* Miz Lollipop. "My daughter won't stop listening to that trash!" she exclaims. "She's only thirteen! I don't want her singing about women's rear ends!"

For some reason, that line sets both me and Amber off, and we burst out laughing together.

"What's so funny?" Fanny demands.

"We've all got rear ends, Fanny," Midge rasps.

The alarm on my cell phone goes off, letting me know it's now 1pm and time to get back to work.

"I guess we'll pick a book next week," Rebecca shrugs. "All right, see you all here next Friday!"

Then she gets up and leaves. Everyone else follows. Except Amber and Samantha, I mean since this is their office.

And, I don't know what does it. Maybe it's the high I got from laughing at poor Fanny Spitzer or the way Amber laughed along with me when Midge brought up the time I fell asleep on the toilet, but I have a sudden rush of confidence. So I approach Amber at her desk.

"Hey, do you want to hang out sometime?"

She just looks at me for a moment, and I suddenly feel nervous. To calm down, in my mind, I play connect-the-dots with the freckles on her face.

"Yeah. Definitely," she says, nodding. "When?"

"I'm free tomorrow evening."

She smiles. "Let's go to Crunchy's Diner. Have you been there?"

I shake my head. "I think I've seen it. It looks nice."

"I was famous there in college."

"You were?" I laugh. "For what?"

"You'll see," she says. Then, she grabs a post-it off her desk, scribbles her phone number on it, and hands it to me. "Call or text me. Let me know when you want to meet up."

"Sounds good, Amber from Tech Support." I smile at her and walk out of her office, feeling better than I've felt in a long time. Like I just drank three more coffees without actually drinking them. I don't even think I'm gonna get the 3pm slump today.

10

JUDIE

Amber bursts through the door of Big Mama's at 4pm.

"Did you get off of work early?"

She shakes her head and forcefully lands on the velvet couch. "Not technically. I just *left*. Samantha doesn't mind doing all the work anyway."

Then, she finally makes eye contact with me.

"I'm still not used to it," she says.

"To what?"

"Your new body. It keeps throwing me off every time I see you."

I've actually been adjusting to my new body quite well. This week, I got some new bras and some more form-fitting T-shirts. I also got a few crop tops and a few dresses, even though it's mid-September, and it's starting to get a little cooler in Chicago. Today, I'm wearing this light grey V-neck sweater-dress that tapers in at my waist.

"Anyway," she continues, "I left early because I wanted to talk to you."

"I wanted to talk to you too!" That's when Luke comes in the front door. He'd been out getting more hazelnut creamer since we ran out this afternoon.

"Hey, Judie," he says, swinging the plastic bag from Jewel at his side. Then he glances at Amber. Well, to be honest, it's more of a glare than a glance. "Hello, Amber. How's my least-favorite customer doing?"

Luke always calls Amber his least-favorite customer because she never pays for anything. I try to tell him that's my fault, but he just laughs at that. I don't think he actually hates Amber that much.

"I'm doing *great*, Luke, because I think I might have a date," she says.

I slam the counter again. "That's fantastic! With Costello?"

Amber rolls her eyes. "No, Judie. I am not dating the forty-five-year-old president of my company. I don't think she even knows my name."

"Yeah," Luke chuckles. "Who would date their *boss*?" He smiles at me when he says it. I'm not sure exactly what that smile's supposed to mean. However, the smile does make me decide to share my news with Amber later tonight at our apartment, rather than right now.

"Wait!" I shout. "Is your date with Kelly from Marketing?"

Amber smiles at that. I like seeing her smile. Lately, I haven't seen her smile much outside of when she's making snarky comments or under the influence.

"I think so," she says.

"What do you mean you *think* so?"

"I mean...I mean, I'm not 100% sure it's a date, is all. We're going to Crunchy's tomorrow—"

"Oh, so you told her—"

"—Yeah, I told her I'm famous there—"

"—Perfect. So how'd you ask her?"

"Well, actually...she asked me."

What! Amber can be so dumb sometimes. I slam the counter again, half in excitement, half instead of smacking Amber's head.

Luke gently pats my shoulder. "Judie, if you keep abusing the counter, I'm going to have to take some money out of your paycheck for repairs." He smiles at me as he says it, though, so I know he doesn't mean it. Which is good because I have no plans to stop slamming the counter.

I stick my tongue out at Luke and come out from behind the counter. I slide onto the armchair across from Amber. "So how'd she ask you?"

"Judie!" Luke calls from behind the counter. "Should I clock you out? Last I checked, gossiping with your sister wasn't in your job description. If it was, you'd own this place by now."

He's still smiling, so I ignore him and look back at Amber. Amber's still smiling, too. It's a happy, happy Friday at Big Mama's Coffee.

"Well," Amber continues, "she just kind of came up to me at the end of our book club meeting—"

I don't have a counter to slam now, so I slap Amber's

knee. She recoils a little. It's for show. Amber's made of steel. "You joined a *book club*?"

"Oh, well, yeah. I thought I told you."

"No you didn't. You didn't tell me, and you didn't *think* you told me. Because you knew I'd make fun of you for joining a book club just to hang out with a cute girl."

"Do we have to focus on her appearance?"

"Yep. So continue. She came up to you after your book club meeting, and?"

Then Amber tells me the rest of the story about how Kelly asked her to hang out, and I squeal excitedly throughout it and occasionally slap various parts of her body. Luke stands behind the counter, rolling his eyes and muttering comments about taking money out of my paycheck.

Later that evening, Amber and I are sitting on our couch, watching *Everybody Loves Raymond* reruns and taking shots every time they make a joke that relies on gender stereotypes. This was Amber and her friend Brianne's favorite game in college.

I'm really just pre-gaming since I'm planning to go out with Michelle and Mikayla tonight. Michelle and Mikayla are my friends from high school. We like to go out to bars and clubs and stuff together every few weeks, just to stay in touch.

"Have you told Brianne yet? About your date?"

Amber shrugs, glancing down at the cell phone in her lap. Damn. She hadn't shrugged all day so far. I was hoping we'd get a world record. "No. We don't really talk about dating and stuff. I have been texting her about this episode of *Everybody Loves Raymond*, though."

I don't know how you can have a best friend and not talk to them about dating. Well, I guess that's what Amber has me for.

Amber sets her phone aside and looks at me. "So, what was your news?"

"My news?"

"Yeah. When I came into Big Mama's today, you said you wanted to talk to me, too."

"Oh, yeah." I smile. "I also have a date tomorrow night!"

Amber slaps my knee at that. (It must run in the family. She just doesn't do as much slapping because she doesn't feel excitement as often as I do.) "With Luke?!"

"No, not with Luke."

"I thought you were interested in Luke!"

I shrug. (Damn. *That* must run in the family, too.) "I am. It's possible to be interested in more than one person at a time."

The look Amber gives me makes me think she's about to mutter one of her quips about *straight girl privilege*, but thankfully, she doesn't. "So who's this date with?" she asks.

"This guy named Ken. He came into Big Mama's this afternoon on his lunch break. He thought I was cute, so he asked me if I wanted to go out tomorrow."

Amber rolls her eyes. I guess whatever high she's on from getting a date with Kelly is wearing off. "Ew, Judie. How can you *like* a guy who hits on you *at work*? When you have *no escape*?"

Now it's *my* turn to roll my eyes. "You're so dramatic, Amber."

She eyes my body up and down. "Well, I guess it makes sense for you to date a Ken. You always were kind of a Barbie. Especially now, with your unrealistically proportioned body."

11

AMBER

It's Saturday night, I'm meeting Kelly in an hour, and I'm so nervous that I'm considering doing something I haven't done since before prom—asking Judie for fashion advice.

Don't get me wrong; I've been on dates and everything. I'm not *that* awkward. I used Tinder in college and all that. I went to the gay bars. I was even three straight girls' "experimentation" phase. I'm not proud of it, but binge drinking makes us do funny things sometimes.

But, I don't know...for some reason I'm a little nervous to go out with Kelly.

I guess part of it is that I'm still not sure if it's a date or not. This could be another Lindsey situation, in which case my back-up plan is to spend all of our future book club meetings hiding in the basement bathroom. Which is kind of a stupid plan since Kelly admitted that's her favorite bathroom too. Even though it's not on her floor.

Also, I assume it will be nothing like it was with Lindsey since Kelly just doesn't seem like the kind of person who'd fool you. I mean, I know I just met her and all, but she kind of radiates sincerity. And perfection. *And shit, I'm already building this girl up.*

When I ask Judie if she can help me find something cute to wear tonight, she just stares at me.

"Amber, your entire wardrobe is two hoodies and a few pairs of jeans. What do you even have to pick from? I'd lend you some of my clothes, but you're too skinny to fit in any of them."

If this had been a month ago, or any other time in our lives really, Judie would be saying that bitterly. But now, it sounds different. When she now says I'm too skinny, it's obvious she's talking down to me. Because *she's* skinny too, now, in her midsection. So she's basically just saying I don't have the tits n' ass to fill out anything new of hers.

Maybe it's meant to be rude—I'm not sure—but she's not telling me anything I don't already know.

But, all of that aside, Judie's still a good sister, which is why her head's currently buried in my closet, thumbing through my meager selection of clothes.

"You have some nice tank tops. Have you shaved your armpits anytime in the last month?" Judie's muffled voice says directly into one of my sweatshirts.

I know that she doesn't want to hear the real answer to that, so I instead I just say, "It's getting a little cold for tank tops."

"Why do you still have band T-shirts from your mid-2000s emo phase?"

"For workout clothes."

Judie pokes her head out of my closet at that. "Do you even work out?"

"No. But I keep them so I can keep telling myself I will one of these days."

"Yeah," Judie nods at me. "You could use some muscle."

Judie has no muscle to speak of, either.

Ten minutes later, I'm standing in front of the bathroom mirror, wearing an unbuttoned blue plaid shirt, a form-fitting white T-shirt, and a pair of skinny jeans. Judie stands next to me, periodically lifting and dropping strands of my hair.

"I'm probably just going to tie it back," I tell her.

"Leave it down," she says. I shrug, and leave it down.

Then I turn to face Judie and lightly punch her shoulder. "Thanks for all your help. Do you want me to help you get ready or anything? For your date with Ken?"

Judie bursts out laughing and exits the bathroom. Hey, I tried.

I check my phone and see that I have only twenty minutes before I'm supposed to meet Kelly. So I load my pockets with my wallet and keys, smoke a third of a joint (it's just a little bit, okay? And I need something to make me less nervous), douse myself in Judie's perfume to cover up the scent, and rush out the door.

Crunchy's Diner has been my favorite restaurant since freshman year of college. They're open 24 hours, which was always perfect when Brianne and I had the 3am drunk munchies. When we first discovered Crunchy's, we were nineteen, underage-drunk for the first time and stumbling through the streets of Chicago looking for somewhere that didn't close at 9pm. Other than, like, McDonald's of course. Brianne got food poisoning there once, so we would avoid fast food. We made a huge scene at Crunchy's when Brianne stole my cell phone to drunk-text my mom. I reached across the booth to wrestle it away from her, and we ended up dropping the phone right into a puddle of barbecue sauce on my plate. After that, every time we'd come to Crunchy's, Oliver, the late-night host, would say, "Oh, it's *you guys* again."

I also liked to go on dates at Crunchy's, the few times I liked a girl from Tinder enough to actually meet up with her. Those were always fun, and it was over the course of one of those dates that I officially became famous at Crunchy's. I don't remember the name of the girl I was with. I guess that was a sign it wasn't meant to be.

Now, I'm sitting in one of the green sparkly plastic booths, sipping some black coffee—which is probably counteracting the effects of the weed I had earlier, but whatever —when I see her come through the front door.

Kelly looks goddamn stunning. While she stands on her toes, searching for me among the booths, the light catches the blue streaks in her hair, and I notice that she's added two more stripes to her bangs.

Kelly's still dressed business casual, even though it's a Saturday. I think business casual might be the only type of clothes she has. She's wearing this blue-and-white striped button-down shirt, with an unbuttoned tight grey sweater on top, and these nice black jeans.

As her eyes dart around the restaurant, I realize I've let her suffer long enough, and I lift my hand to wave to her. She acknowledges me with a big smile and a nod and heads over to my booth.

"This place is so cute!" she exclaims, sliding in across from me.

"Yeah. It's my favorite place to go for...with...to hang out." What do I say there? To go for dates? To go with new friends? *You're going to have to figure this out sooner or later,* I tell myself. But for now I just shut myself up with another sip of coffee.

"Do they have good coffee here?" she asks, and I almost choke a little trying to swallow too fast so I can answer.

"Yeah. Sorry I went ahead and ordered some before you got here."

"Oh, no problem at all. I've only had one cup of coffee today and I desperately need some more."

Once we both have coffee, we get started on looking through the five-page laminated menu, and I realize that we're both terrible at small talk. So I continue to stare at the menu, even though I always order the same thing here.

Thankfully, Kelly breaks the silence. "So, wait, why are you famous here?"

I look up from my menu at her. She's smiling expectantly. I chuckle to myself. "Bottom of page four."

Kelly flips to page four, and an even bigger smile breaks out on her face. "Woah! And that's because of you?"

I nod. "Yep."

Page four has the burger list. The last burger on the list is called The Amber, and yes, it's named after me.

The Amber is a double burger with a layer of crushed Fritos in between the two patties, drenched in barbecue sauce, and topped with fried pickles. The first time I custom-ordered this burger was five years ago, one of the times Brianne and I were too drunk to function. It was so delicious, I ordered that exact burger every time I came to Crunchy's from then on.

One night, after an otherwise unmemorable Tinder date, Oliver grabbed me by my sleeve on my way out. "Amber, right?" he said.

"Yeah," I said, avoiding eye contact because this was one of those times that I was trying to hide how high I was.

"Me and a few of the guys in the kitchen were talking, and we want to add that burger you always order to the menu."

I got so excited then, which was probably at least partially because of the weed I'd most likely had that night, that I leapt off the ground and took Oliver into a big hug.

So I named the burger the Amber Alert, and it became their third-best-selling specialty burger. But then a bunch of soccer moms (like the skinny white yuppie types from the soy chip commercial) protested the Amber Alert burger because the name was "offensive." They almost boycotted Crunchy's because of it.

Crunchy's daytime clientele is mostly skinny moms and their chubby kids, so Crunchy's changed the name of my burger to just "The Amber." Burger + controversy = instant fame. So I'm kinda famous at Crunchy's now.

So I tell Kelly this story, and she's laughing her head off the entire time.

Then, feeling confident, I put my elbows on the table and lean forward a little. "So. Are you gonna try it?"

"Well, to be honest, I'm a vegetarian," she says, still smiling. "But I'd be happy to try it with a veggie burger instead."

Of course Kelly's a vegetarian. I swear, she's basically a Disney princess. Like *Snow White* or something. But not the soft, gentle Disney version of Snow White. Like a *sexy* Snow White. Like, who knows what she was doing with those seven men she lived with? Then I stop that train of thought because I do *not* want to think about Kelly with men.

We wait a few minutes for our food. I watch Kelly's nails—still painted dark green and silver—as they absent-mindedly tap the outside of her white coffee mug.

Kelly's first bite of The Amber is anti-climactic. She just scrunches up her nose a little, then starts softly giggling into the burger. "Amber," she says, her mouth full of chewed-up burger and half-giggles, "this burger is gross."

By the time she takes her second bite, I'm already halfway through mine. "Your taste is gross, Kelly from Marketing," I answer, laughing along with her. "If you eat the whole thing, I'll pay for dinner."

Kelly rolls her eyes. "Fine. You drive a hard bargain, Amber from Tech Support."

Okay. So I've established that I'm paying for dinner.

That's +1 for this being a date, right? And the way she keeps smiling and giggling and stuff...that's *gotta* be flirting, right? But I just have this annoying voice gnawing at the back of my head. (That voice's name is *Fucking Lindsey.*) I guess I should do *something* to figure out where we stand. At least before I get too invested.

I chug the rest of my coffee for some last-minute confidence. "Listen up, Kelly from Marketing!" I announce, punctuating my statement with the slam of my coffee cup against the table.

Kelly makes perfect eye contact with me, her smile never fading.

"We're just getting to know each other. So after I pay, we're going to take a walk through Chicago, and we're going to play a game."

Her smile widens again.

God, that smile could kill me. I bet kittens send each other internet memes of Kelly's smile. It's *that* cute.

"What kind of game?"

"The kind of game where we ask each other questions, and have to answer honestly. Like truth or dare, or something."

"All right," says Kelly, leaning toward me again. "I'm in."

I'm sure hoping this is a date because if it is, it's the best one I've ever had.

12

KELLY

I'M NOT SURE WHERE I GOT THIS ABILITY TO SAY THINGS with 100% conviction, while still having no idea what the fuck I'm doing.

But Amber wants to play truth or dare in the streets of Chicago, and what the hell, I'm going to do it.

"Truth or dare?" I ask Amber as we stroll east out of the West Loop.

"Dare."

The first thing that comes to mind is one of those "Chicago things" that Rebecca told me about when I first moved here. "On the way home, I dare you to steal one of those maps out of the 'L' train."

"Oh, so we're going home together, then?"

Fuck. I didn't think about that. Are we? I can feel my heartbeat in my ears, and I'm silently praying that Amber can't hear it. So I just say, "Sure, why not?" and it comes out flirty and confident, even though I'm 90% sure I heard my voice crack halfway through.

We reach one of those bridges over the river, and we start walking along it. To our right, cars zip by, and above our heads, a Green Line train speeds by, shaking the wooden planks under our feet.

"Truth or dare, Kelly?" Amber stops walking and stares out at the river. I stand next to her.

"Truth."

The breath she takes is so deep I can hear it. "Is this a date?" She whips her head around and stares right at me. I try to read her eyes, but I can't.

"Did you want it to be?" When I say that, it sounds cute, like in a teasing sort of way. But inside, I'm cringing. Who answers a question with another question?

She doesn't answer. She just keeps her eyes locked on my face, and slowly, she nods.

I move a little closer to her, so we're standing shoulder-to-shoulder by the railing overlooking the river. I exhale and drop my voice to a whisper. "Then it is."

She leans in a little more, until our lips are touching.

And the next thing I know, we're making out on a Chicago River bridge. Her face smells like a fruity perfume (which I never would've guessed), and she still kind of tastes like that super gross burger. That thought makes me start laughing.

I'm laughing into another girl's mouth.

Holy shit, could I *get* any more awkward?

She pulls away then. "What's so funny?"

"You still taste like that gross burger." (I can't believe I said that out loud.)

But she just starts laughing, too. Then, she grabs my hand and runs across the bridge, pulling me along with her.

When we get back to my apartment, the first thing I do is hang the map Amber stole off the Brown Line on my wall with a thumb tack, right in the middle of my art.

Amber sits in my armchair, holding Sienna in her lap. "Your art's beautiful," she says. "Your cat paintings, especially." She strokes Sienna's fur while I step back to admire the placement of the "L" train map among the rest of my art. "But why is Harry Potter making out with Draco Malfoy in that one?" She points to a sketch on the right side of the wall.

"Don't think too hard about it," I answer because how else do you answer that?

I sit cross-legged on the floor across from her. She scoots over in the armchair and pats the empty space next to her. Sienna, who has now fallen asleep in Amber's lap, doesn't flinch.

So I squeeze onto the chair next to Amber.

"Truth or dare?" she asks, her eyes focused on Sienna curled up in her lap.

"Truth."

"Why do you work in marketing?"

"Two reasons. One because it's one of the only ways to regularly get paid for my art. Two because I can afford this apartment."

"Fair enough."

"How about you? Why do you work in tech support?"

She shrugs. "To pay the bills, I guess. I don't want to stay there forever."

I stare at Sienna, watching her little tummy expand and deflate as she breathes. "Where would you like to end up?"

"I guess it sounds kinda stupid, but...I don't know. I'd like to do something that makes an impact. Like, right now, sometimes I do some freelance writing for *The Feminist Forum*, but that barely pays anything. Maybe if I put something out there that really took off, and got a lot of people thinking...then I could do some real work for social change."

I nod. "I believe in you."

"Thanks," she says, smiling. Then, she leans her head against my shoulder, and we rock back and forth a little in the armchair, while she continues to pet Sienna.

I'm glad we decided this is a date because it's one of the best ones I've ever had.

13

JUDIE

THIS IS THE WORST DATE I'VE EVER BEEN ON.

Ken is what some teenage girls would refer to as "a fuck boy."

I'm not sure if I should text Amber about this, for two reasons. One, she's on a date of her own, and it's probably going a thousand times better than mine is, so I don't want to impose. And two, she *warned* me against going out with a guy who would ask me out at work. So if I tell her how awful Ken is, she's just going to be all smug about it.

But I'm hiding in the bathroom at Venice Blues, this pretty, upscale Italian restaurant in the West Loop. The *bathrooms* are nicer than most of my apartment. I could just hide in this stall all night. But it would be so much more fun to have Amber here, so we could cry in the bathroom together, like at prom.

Also, I feel sort of lame for just ditching Ken. But if I had to listen to him talk about himself for another minute, I would've gone *insane.*

Ken is a stock broker. I don't know what a stock broker does, and I don't particularly care. I'm sure Ken told me all about what a stock broker does, in excruciating detail, but I had to tune him out after about five minutes before my brain exploded.

I tried to talk to him about things that interest *me*, too. Like sitcoms, and fashion, and pop music, and making lattes. But I struggled to get a word in edgewise, and that's saying something because I *never* struggle to get a word in.

The worst part was that I don't think Ken was even interested in hearing about me at all. He just wanted to sound impressive enough to get me to go home with him. I could tell because he stared at my boobs the whole night.

On the one hand, I don't blame the guy. I do have *fantastic* boobs now. On the other hand, that doesn't mean I'm a prostitute you can buy with fettuccine alfredo.

Though, on the plus side, I don't have to feel guilty about eating giant plates of fettuccine alfredo anymore. If I gain any weight, I can just move it to my butt.

As I was eating my amazing pasta (it really was amazing —I'll have to get Amber and Michelle and Mikayla to take me here for my twenty-third birthday this February), Ken just kept spouting off all these stats about his income and his apartment, clearly trying to get me to agree to go there with him.

Things like, "When I got my Christmas bonus last year, the first thing I did was install a hot tub on my balcony."

And, "Sometimes I hate the long hours at work, but I love that I can afford to live right in the heart of downtown."

And even, "My apartment is really beautiful. You should see it. You would love it. Would you like to see it?"

If I tried to talk about sitcoms or something, he'd say, "If all goes well, we won't have any time for watching sitcoms *tonight.*" Or if I tried to bring up that I like Miz Lollipop, he'd say something like, "Oh yeah. What's that new song? 'Worship Dat Booty.' I know someone that could apply to."

I guess I feel kind of like a hypocrite, too. I didn't know *anything* about Ken when I agreed to go on a date with him. I just said yes because he had a welcoming smile, and I liked the way the light bounced off his grey eyes.

So, all I knew about him was that he was hot. And that's all he knew about me, too. I guess I was just idealistic enough to think that maybe we'd get along as people, too. I wasn't so lucky this time.

I'll have to vet my guys better in the future.

Instead of facing my problems head-on like an adult, I'm still hiding in a bathroom stall, hoping that if enough time goes by, Ken will get the hint and just leave.

Also, this bathroom is really nice. The flushers on the toilets are *gold.* I'm sure they're not *real* gold, but they're at least painted a convincing shade of gold. And the sinks are giant bowls with automatic soap dispensers. *And* there's a couch right outside the stalls. I'm not sitting on the couch because there's already a group of mildly drunk girls on that couch, and the inside of the stalls are almost as nice.

I'm wondering if I should try to find a window in the bathroom and escape through it. Isn't that what girls do in rom-coms when their dates go badly? Or during a wacky montage?

But this bathroom is too *posh* to have a window. It's too

pristine white and too full of mood lighting. Plus, if I tried to sneak out a window, I'm worried my boobs would get stuck.

I end up staying in the bathroom for about an hour, at which point I poke my head out of the door, scan the restaurant for Ken, and see that he's finally gone. Then I rush home.

Around midnight, Amber gets home and finds me lying on the couch, eating mint chocolate chip ice cream out of the tub. (I can do this all I want now!)

"I'm guessing it didn't go well?" she says, gesturing to the ice cream.

I shake my head. "But I'm guessing yours did. Based on the fact that you're just getting home now."

Amber slides onto the couch, squeezing into the little space between my feet and the left armrest. "It was fantastic, actually. But yours sucked, so you first." She grabs the spoon from my hand and eats some ice cream off of it.

"Just try not to be smug about it, okay?"

"Who, me? I'm *never* smug."

I pick up a pillow from the couch and hit her in the face with it. "No I-told-you-sos, okay?"

She nods.

"Ken wasn't really interested in me. Just my new body. He didn't even make eye contact with me *once*. I was like, hello, I'm trying to *talk* to you. Maybe I should get another Lipamorph pill and move all the fat to my eyes."

Amber's eyes grow wide in horror. "You should *what*?"

"It was a joke."

Then, she bursts out laughing. "Oh my god. I'm just

imagining that in real life. Like you with these big, obese, bulging *eyeballs*."

And then I start laughing too, and Amber and I spend the rest of the night eating ice cream and laughing, while she tells me about Kelly from Marketing.

And I feel like everything's going to be okay.

14

AMBER

It feels weird admitting I was wrong. But, nonetheless, I was wrong. I was wrong when I thought I hated everything about marketing. Because let me tell you, I really, *really* like Kelly from Marketing.

Almost every night, I text Kelly while I watch sitcoms with Judie. Sometimes, Kelly watches along too, from her apartment. Sometimes she doesn't, and she just teases me about how much time I waste watching sitcoms, and then goes back to making gorgeous art and reinventing the wheel and curing cancer and whatever other amazing things Kelly does in her spare time.

Every day during our lunch break (except Friday), I meet her in that basement bathroom outside my office suite, and we make out in the stall farthest from the sink. No one else has come in yet. Not even Midge the janitor.

On Friday, we meet in my basement office room for our book club meetings, along with Rebecca, Samantha, Isabelle, Fanny, Tanya, and Midge. Despite it being our second book club meeting, we still don't pick a book by the time the lunch break is up. We just spend the entire time gossiping and comparing lunches.

At one point, while Midge is sharing her family's secret hummus recipe with us, Kelly leans over and lightly kisses my cheek. In front of six other people. I didn't know if we were official enough yet to show affection in front of other people, but leave it to Kelly to make the bold and confident moves I'm too nervous to make myself.

Then, after work, we run around Chicago together—holding hands and everything. Just running around the Windy City, letting brown and yellow leaves fall all over us and get stuck in our hair. Somehow, Kelly looks even *more* gorgeous with her hair all full of fallen leaves—like she's some kind of fairy or flower child or something. Damn.

We lie on the grass in Millennium Park together and look at clouds. She kisses me next to the Buckingham Fountain. I legitimately feel like I'm in a romantic comedy or something. But maybe, like a satirical, futuristic rom-com since Judie's new body is still making me feel like we're in the Twilight Zone.

And I guess it's not just Judie's body, either. Since I've learned about Lipamorph, I feel like I've been seeing more and more women with these perfectly proportioned curvy bodies. Maybe it's just that I'm looking for it now. But I could've sworn that, at our book club meeting earlier today, Isabelle looked a little fuller in the chest than usual. Not that I was *intentionally* looking at her that way—she's like nineteen, at most.

All that aside, Kelly and I are having a fantastic Friday

evening adventure around Chicago. We stop at this vegetarian food truck, which she forces me to try since last week she, in her words, "ate that gross burger for *you*, Amber!"

So I try this weird-ass seaweed wrap, and it's actually pretty good. But that might be because I'll eat just about anything.

Then, without even talking about it, we just hop on the Purple Line, catching one of the last express trains out of the Loop, and head to Kelly's apartment.

And *this* time, we're making out before we even get the front door locked behind us, and Kelly's hands are in my hair, and we even briefly crash into the kitchen sink. Kelly tastes like peppermint—cool, clean, sweet. Then, the next thing we know—and I don't even remember entering a new room—we're lying on her bed.

Now she's on top of me. She's taken her glasses off and set them on the bedside table, and I can stare directly into her eyes. Green, with flecks of gold and brown splattered around the pupils. Long eyelashes, leading up to black eyebrows.

She kisses twice down my neck, then rolls off of me and lies at my side, facing me.

I realize I'm breathing way heavier than normal, so I take a second to calm myself down.

"You've, uh...you've done this before, right?" she asks.

I nod. "Haven't you?"

"I—I mean...I don't know."

Jesus Christ. On top of everything else, Kelly can't be a virgin too. It's just too much. I'm expecting little bunnies and deer to just start flocking around her, and little blue birds to land on her shoulder. I wonder if that's ever happened to her in real life. I wouldn't be surprised.

So I answer, "What do you mean you don't know?"

"I mean...I've only ever done this—like, sex, I mean—with one other person. And I dated him for a year before I did it."

"Him?"

She nods. "My ex-boyfriend, Zack. We dated for three years in college."

"So you mean, that this is, like, the first time you've been with a girl then?"

Kelly nods, not once breaking eye contact. "Yeah. But it's not a big deal. I've known I was bisexual since, like, high school."

I break eye contact with her to lie on my back and stare up at the ceiling. "I didn't know that. That you also like guys, I mean."

"Yeah," she says. "That's okay, right?"

I don't know how to answer that. I mean, *of course* it's okay. I can't judge a woman based on whether or not she's had a dick in her before. That goes against *everything* I believe as a feminist. But at the same time, I guess I'm kind of surprised she didn't tell me.

So that's my answer. "Of course it's okay. But why didn't you tell me?"

"I guess I didn't think it was relevant."

"...Fair enough."

"So do you, uh...do you want to get back to..."

"Yes."

When we're done, I'm lying in a sweaty heap on top of Kelly. Some of the bed sheets have fallen off the side of the bed, and Sienna's aggressively clawing at them.

Kelly's mouth creeps up right next to my ear. "Do you want to shower?" she whispers, her breath tickling my skin.

I just nod. We both ignore the cat.

I guess this is a first for me, too, since I've never showered with anyone before. The hot water hits my skin, and I watch the steam fog up the glass door. Kelly draws a smiley face in the fog. I briefly consider drawing a heart with our initials in it or something, but then I almost gag at that idea. That's something that would happen in one of Judie's romance novels, not in my real life.

Kelly stands directly under the shower head, letting the stream of hot water soak her hair. Her bangs flatten and start to fall into her eyes.

I see streams of mascara fall down her cheeks. I guess I'd never thought about whether or not Kelly wore makeup before. (I don't.) I guess it makes sense that she does, since it goes with her artsy personality. And I could definitely see her wearing dark red lipstick sometime. (That would be hot as hell.)

She leans forward and kisses me, and for a second, we just press our bodies together and let the hot water envelop us.

Then, when she pulls back, all of her make-up has come off.

And my heart skips a beat, but not in a good way this time. I'm suddenly super nervous, and I feel something turning around in my stomach.

She still looks pretty, don't get me wrong. Kelly could lose half her face and still look pretty. But she looks *different.*

And then my heart rate speeds up, and I start thinking way too many thoughts at once. Like how until an hour ago, I didn't know that Kelly was a girl who also fucks guys. *Just one guy,* I try to remind myself. *And you're not going to judge her for that since it goes against everything you believe as a feminist. Even if the thought of Kelly with a guy makes you think of Fucking Lindsey and her gross hipster-ass fiancé.*

And now I'm staring at her pale face (still pretty, of course), and thinking about how she looked so much better a few seconds ago, before all the make-up washed off. But it's not a big deal, I remind myself because *you'd never judge another girl based on her appearance. And regardless, her appearance is still fantastic.*

But, my stupid mind interjects, *you can't think a girl is prettier with makeup on. Especially not a girl you're attracted to. That goes against everything you believe as a feminist.*

As my breath picks up a little, I realize I need to get out of here before I say something I regret. I'm not always known for having the best filter. Just ask Judie.

So I just mumble, "Sorry," and slide the shower door open.

Still soaking wet, I pull my red hoodie on over my head

and slide my jeans on. Since I'm still dripping, my jeans stick to my legs, and it's a struggle to pull them up. I slide my sneakers on without any socks, and run out.

As I race to the "L," wind whipping through my cold, wet hair and making me shiver, I try not to think about the confused look on Kelly's face as I ran away.

15

JUDIE

"I HATE MEN!" I ANNOUNCE AS I WALK THROUGH THE front door to my apartment on Friday evening.

"Glad you finally realized it," Amber says, her voice monotone.

I look down and see Amber lying on the hardwood floor of our living room. Her hair is soaking wet and splayed out all around her, and her red hoodie is soaked with wet spots all down the sides.

"What happened to you?" I ask.

She shrugs. (What else is new.) Then, she cranes her neck, so she's facing me upside down from the floor. "Did your boobs get even bigger, or is that the angle?"

I look down at my chest, which has, in fact, gotten bigger. "I took an extra pill this morning," I tell her.

She sits up cross-legged on the floor. "You don't think that's dangerous?"

"Says the girl who's high more often than not." I sit on the floor across from her.

"That's not even true, Judie. I smoke weed like twice a

week at most. Plus, it's not like there's anything *dangerous* about what I'm doing."

"What's dangerous about Lipamorph?" I counter. "The only side effects are nausea, vomiting, and dry eyes, and I've experienced *none* of those—"

"What's *dangerous*," Amber says, glaring into my eyes, "is that you're taking a drug that lets men objectify you."

"Excuse me?"

"Sorry if I made an incorrect assumption. But I assume the reason you came in here announcing that you hate men isn't because you've decided to bat for my team, Judie. I assume you had another awful date like the one last weekend with Ken."

Shit. We must have some kind of sister mind-connection because she's 100% right. Today, I went out with a guy named Josh that I met on Tinder. I tried to vet my dates better, like I promised myself last week. We talked in the Tinder chat about lots of things ahead of time, like sitcoms and pop music and lattes—all the things I *couldn't* talk about with Ken.

But Josh was the same. He was just humoring me because he was impressed by my boobs.

And yes, I did take an extra pill this morning. It's not that I thought I *needed* to make myself look sexier, but...I don't know. I thought maybe Josh and I would have a lot in common, and I *really* wanted to look my best on our first date.

Then, when I finally met him, it's like he forgot he even had any interest in the things I like. All he wanted to do was pound back whiskey sours at the bar, then take me back to his apartment. He was even less subtle than Ken; half his sentences were innuendos.

"You're right, Amber." I stand up and dust off my butt. "I did have a shitty date. But I didn't *ask* for Josh to objectify me."

"Then why are you taking a pill whose sole purpose is to give women easy access to the body types *men* most desire?"

"I take it for *myself*," I nearly shout. Amber and I haven't had an argument this heated in months. "I take it because *I* want to have confidence in the way I look."

"Well," she spits, "when they way you want to look is *exactly* the body type that the media and advertisements have been telling us for *decades* is the body *men* want, then don't be surprised when your body is *all* they want."

I stare at her for a moment. Then, I make perfect eye contact with her, before I drop my bomb. "Isn't that victim blaming?"

She just stares at me for a second. I don't think she knew I had that kind of argument in me.

So I just keep going. "I've listened to enough of your feminist theory over my twenty-two years as your sister. I know victim blaming when I hear it. What about women who *naturally* have a body that looks like this? Hmm? Are they *asking for it*, Amber?"

She leaps to her feet then, and looks me directly in the eyes. I can almost see fire growing in her irises.

"You're right Judie," she says, though it really doesn't sound like she's ready to concede. "You're *right*. I'm a hypocrite, and a misogynist, and a terrible fucking girlfriend."

"I never said—"

"You didn't need to! It's nothing I don't already know." Then she turns and storms off to her bedroom, slamming the door behind her.

Then it hits me. Amber probably had a shitty date, too.

We really *do* have some weird sister connection.

16

AMBER

When I finish my fight with Judie, my mind's so jumbled that all I can do is hole myself up in my room and try to calm down. I briefly consider listening to some Eminem since that's prime anger-management music, but I know Judie will hear it in the next room, and everyone with ears knows Eminem's a hardcore misogynist, so I'll just be proving all of Judie's points more.

So instead, I just throw on a pair of baggy grey sweatpants and a worn-in West Loop College sweatshirt, and flop on my bed.

Victim blaming. Honestly, I didn't know Judie had that kind of argument in her. And I feel bad, I do because I do underestimate her a lot more often than I should. Judie's smarter than anyone likes to give her credit for.

And, in this case, she's *right*.

But that's not what it's even about—it's not about winning or losing an argument with my sister. I'm starting to think this Lipamorph business is bigger than either or us. Even bigger than the sum of us together. And I'm wondering if I should resign myself to the fact that

Lipamorph *is* going to be a part of our lives, whether I like it or not.

So I spend the rest of the evening lying on my bed, my hot laptop balanced on my stomach, reading *The Feminist Forum*. I haven't written a new post for them in a while, but there's been a gnawing feeling in the back of my head, like maybe I should start a new one soon. But right now, I just type "lipamorph" in the search bar.

I guess part of me needs to read other people's opinions in order to contextualize my own.

Maybe that makes me a shitty feminist. But Judie's already made it clear that's what I am, so what do I have to lose?

Leave it to The Feminist Forum *to always be on top of its game*, I think to myself, as hundreds of results appear on my laptop screen.

"Legalization of Lipamorph a Victory for Feminism," the top headline reads. The article then goes on to describe how women having full control over the way their bodies look is a step in the right direction for freedom and bodily autonomy. It makes a salient point, I must admit. But something still doesn't sit right with me.

The next headline hits the nail on the head:

"Loathing Lipamorph: the Drug that Pressures Women into Subscribing to Patriarchal Beauty Standards."

If I'm being honest, the first thing I think upon reading that headline is, *that is way too long for a headline*. But if my experience writing for *The Feminist Forum* is anything to go by, the person who wrote it was paid only $25 for the whole article, so I'm not judging too hard.

I check the name of the author. Alice Gilbert. I don't know any Alice Gilberts, at least that I'm aware of. But Alice Gilbert and I seem to think the same way because her article is *spot on.*

It starts off with Alice discussing her hatred of marketing: how women's bodies are used to target male consumers since it's still some kind of unspoken rule that men are the ones earning the money. Then she discusses how ads and the media try to sell a body to women. Thin, smooth, and soft, but with fat *where it counts.* In the places where men most want it. *It's just evolution,* straight men will argue. *We're biologically programmed to like tits n' ass because back when we were cavemen, it was the easiest way to tell who was most fertile.*

Because that's the other unspoken rule: that all women are is eye candy and baby cannons.

"Life imitates art, and art imitates life," Alice Gilbert argues, paraphrasing Plato.

I don't know much about art, I think to myself. *I'll have to ask Kelly what she thinks.*

Then, of course, I have to stop reading for a second because I get a tight pain in my stomach from thinking about Kelly. How I just left her standing in the shower, weirdly gawking at me as I ran from her apartment, half-dressed and dripping wet. The confusion in her eyes as she struggled to understand a fear that I'm not sure I understand yet myself.

The fact that I may have fucked up the greatest thing that's ever happened to me.

Was it the greatest thing that ever happened to you? My mind's in the mood to argue with me. *Why do you think a relationship is the greatest thing that's ever happened to you? Isn't the concept of a relationship as a woman's biggest accomplishment—regardless of whether it's a same-sex relationship—isn't that just another lie that marketing sells to women? And doesn't Kelly work in marketing?*

Or, deep down, do we all just want to be loved?

I exhale heavily. I'm not even high yet and already getting way too deep.

On the laptop screen in front of me, Alice Gilbert continues explaining how life imitates art. How culture is built from the images we see around us.

"In the past," she explains, "we could watch a pop star in a music video or read a Victoria's Secret catalog, and feel a brief pang of jealousy. But then we'd move on because we saw the normal women around us. Our mothers, our sisters, our friends. Ladies who didn't have those bodies. And by relegating those bodies as something for the elite, we could take comfort in knowing that our imperfections were normalized. With easy access to Lipamorph, perfection is becoming normalized instead. Nowadays, we all have no excuse *not* to be perfect. And God forbid we don't want to be."

I think in real life, Alice Gilbert and I would be friends.

And I guess all of this is what I want to tell Judie; that she's allowing herself to be manipulated by other people's (especially men's) standard of perfect, when she should feel perfect the way she is.

Of course, I don't know how to tell her this.

I also don't know how to tell Kelly what I was feeling earlier. Why I panicked. I don't know where to even begin.

So I don't. I just slink further down in my bed and watch some lesbian accountant porn until I fall asleep. Happy Friday.

17

AMBER

The following Saturday, I text Kelly something to the effect of, "I'm so sorry, I don't know what came over me. I must've panicked because it was my first time ever showering with another person." It's at least a partial truth, so I deem it okay.

We meet up for coffee on Sunday at Big Mama's. It's nice. A calm date, with no pressure. A perfect contrast to the last time we saw each other.

Apparently, Kelly's always wanted to try Big Mama's since she lives only a few blocks away. Since Judie's the only one working here at the moment, we convince her to give us both a free latte.

I don't bring up any of the stuff I read on *The Feminist Forum*, or my fight with Judie, or my concerns about the growing popularity of Lipamorph. (Seriously, just on the bus ride over here, I counted four women with perfect hourglass bodies. And those were just the ones who were standing up.) None of that stuff is what we should be talking about today, not after I almost bombed our whole relationship on Friday evening. Today's for chilling and getting to know each other.

For example, I learn that Kelly loves a good pumpkin spice latte, just like every other young urban professional I know.

"I know, I can be a stereotype sometimes," she admits with a laugh.

She convinces me to try a pumpkin spice latte as well since, in her words, "You still owe me for that gross burger I ate on our first date."

"When will that debt finally be repaid?" I ask, crossing my legs on the velvet couch and taking a sip from my white mug.

"I don't know. We'll see," she smiles. "Maybe never. I can't guarantee anything."

As much as I don't want to be stuck eating Kelly's vegetarian food and drinking flavored lattes forever, I have to admit, the dynamic between us feels nice. Like it did last week. Like we could go right back to making out in the basement bathroom at work tomorrow. Like I never had a stupid freak-out and ran out of the shower like a weirdo.

Judie's right; I *can* be dramatic sometimes.

Monday at work, Kelly and I are still good. I spend most of my shift spinning around in my chair and texting her links to goofy YouTube videos I find. Every time, she responds with some quip about how she has a job to be doing, but I know she does watch them because within a half hour she'll always respond with some joke about whatever video I just sent her.

What I like about Kelly is that it's starting to feel as easy as it did with Brianne. Not that Brianne and I ever dated or anything. But, for the first time since college, I finally feel like I have a best friend. A best friend that I'm dating.

I'm in love with my best friend.

I'm living the dream, aren't I?

Suddenly, I stop spinning in my chair. *Am I in love with Kelly?* We haven't said "I love you" to each other yet. I mean, it would be kind of ridiculous to since our first date was only a week and a half ago.

Judie used to warn me not to fall in love too fast. But Judie's failed relationships were different, I think. Kelly's not like anyone I've ever met before.

Isn't that what all the poets and the songwriters and the soccer moms say? That when you fall in love, you just *know*?

At our book club meeting on Friday, we still don't pick a book. I'm not sure if we're ever going to actually read anything. But we're all making new friends, which is what Kelly tells me was Rebecca's real goal when she started this whole thing, anyway.

Rebecca herself doesn't even seem all that interested in picking a book. She spends the first ten minutes of our meeting raving about how the Cubs won last night, and the Bears are probably going to win on Sunday, and how her fiancé, Quentin, got her season tickets for the Bulls for her birthday. I don't think Rebecca ever thinks about anything other than

Chicago and making new friends. Well, and marketing, I guess, since she works with Kelly. It must be really nice to live inside Rebecca's head. It seems like a happy place. Other than the whole having-to-work-in-marketing thing, I mean.

Like usual, we're all just sitting on the floor in a circle and talking about random stuff. Occasionally, someone will suggest a book for all of us to read, and we'll nod along and say, "Yeah, that sounds good." But inside, we all know that we're going to forget to read it. I've got my mid-2000s alternative rock playlist blasting from YouTube on my computer in the background. It's nice.

Then, of course, Miz Lollipop's Lipamorph commercial comes on as one of the ads between songs.

Fanny Spitzer rolls her eyes. "I hate that Mrs. Lollipop," she says. "What she makes isn't even real music, and it's corrupting our children."

I swear, Fanny Spitzer talks like a parody of a 1950s Christian housewife. Even though I'm not a fan of Miz Lollipop either, I still have to fight back the urge to laugh at Fanny.

"Fanny, that's racist," Tanya cuts in. "Miz Lollipop is a strong woman who's unashamed of her sexuality. To call her 'corrupt' just further dismisses the empowerment of black women. And by saying her music isn't 'real,' you're kind of dissing black culture as a whole."

"It's not about race, honey," Fanny says condescendingly. (To be fair, pretty much everything Fanny says comes out condescendingly. It might be her voice.) "I just don't think a woman who makes money by screaming about her rear end deserves to be called an artist."

"She *is* an artist," says Tanya. "Have you ever actually *listened* to her songs? The rhythm, the meter, the internal rhyme schemes? Whether you like her subject matter or not, Miz Lollipop is a *poet*."

I should introduce Tanya to Judie. I think they'd be friends. Although I don't think Judie spends time thinking about Miz Lollipop's *internal rhyme scheme* or anything like that. I think she just likes to dance to it while she drinks cocktails.

Despite the Lipamorph commercial being long over and the alt-rock playlist continuing like nothing happened, our book club continues to argue about Miz Lollipop and whether she's a feminist icon or degrading to women.

At first, I don't think I should bring up my opinion on Miz Lollipop. Because it's kind of in the middle of these two roads. I agree with Tanya that she's cool and empowered in owning her body. At the same time...I'm still kind of bitter about her whole "not in a gay way" thing. And then since we all know my filter isn't great, I'd probably end up launching into a rant about Fucking Lindsey, and I don't think Kelly would be too pleased to listen to that.

But then, I *do* interject. I don't know why. Maybe it's because of my aforementioned nonexistent filter. Maybe it's because I'm sick of listening to Fanny and Tanya throw the same arguments back and forth at each other. Either way, I can't be blamed for what comes out of my mouth next. "What about the commercial she's in, though?"

Everyone stops talking and looks at me. "I mean, if we look beyond her music. What do you think about Lipamorph? About the fact that she creates her own body with a pill? That like she, and Betty J, and all these other women are doing that?"

Tanya shrugs. "I think it's great. I haven't tried Lipamorph yet myself, but honestly, I've considered it. If it gives women more confidence, I'm all for it."

"I like it, too" a soft voice squeaks.

We all whip our heads around to look at Isabelle, sitting cross-legged on the floor. Her honey-blonde hair is tied back in a ponytail, with two escaped strands framing her face. I was right; her chest *is* bigger.

"I've been using it for a week now. Personally, I like it. All my life, people have thought I'm younger than I am. I still get carded at *PG-13 movies* sometimes."

This surprises none of us. Isabelle could pass for twelve if you think hard enough about it.

She continues. "Last spring, when I started interning here, Vivian Costello thought I was someone's daughter on take-your-kid-to-work day. People don't believe me when I tell them I'm nineteen. And when people think you're still a preteen, no one takes you seriously. So I gave myself a more grown-up body."

I cringe a little at that. The way she says "grown-up body" kind of makes her sound like she's *actually* twelve.

"And now," she continues, "people notice me. Vivian Costello tells me I'm doing a good job and gives me more responsibilities. She's even talked about interviewing me for a full-time position after I graduate in a few years. So, personally, I'm thankful for it."

"That's sad," I say quietly.

"What's sad about it?" asks Midge. "I'm glad Isabelle finally feels accepted in the workplace. You go, honey!"

When Midge says "honey," it sounds *totally* different from when Fanny says it. Maybe because Midge always sounds like she's just chain-smoked three packs of cigarettes. And because she's usually saying something encouraging, not something condescending.

"It's sad," I say, "because Isabelle shouldn't have *had* to alter her body to be taken seriously. Maybe I'm the only one who feels this way, but personally, I don't like Lipamorph. It's giving women even more pressure than before to adhere to patriarchal beauty standards."

"But how is it different from something like plastic surgery?" Tanya asks. "Honestly, people have been able to alter their body for decades. This is just a new—and honestly, safer—way to do it."

"Because," Samantha interjects. "Plastic surgery is expensive. It's something only the wealthy can afford. By making this 'perfect' body available to the masses, it completely normalizes it, and takes it from an *ideal* to an *expectation*."

I stare at Samantha for a moment. I don't think I've ever heard her talk before, other than when she's answering the phone calls I ignore. But she's saying *exactly* what I'm thinking.

"Yes. That's exactly my point," I tell Samantha. "I'm

worried about my sister. She's taking it nonstop. She feels better about herself, sure. And men are *constantly* noticing her. But she's having trouble finding the guys who like her for *her*, rather than her body."

"But her body is a *part* of her now," says Tanya. "Dating is difficult no matter what drugs you take or what your body looks like."

"Plus, Amber," Midge says with a wink, "you got yourself the prettiest girl here. And you didn't have to alter *shit*."

That's when I glance at Kelly, sitting on my left. And I realize that throughout the entire meeting, she hasn't said a word.

18

KELLY

Well. I guess there's another thing I'll *NEVER* be telling Amber.

19

AMBER

SATURDAY MORNING, I WAKE UP THINKING ABOUT THE argument we had yesterday at the book club meeting, and I'm feeling...inspired, I guess. Energized. Charged. Like maybe I'm finally ready to start another article for *The Feminist Forum*. And then use the $25 I make to take Kelly on a nice date.

Kelly and I have plans this afternoon to explore the campus of West Loop College since she'd never even heard of it before me. I don't blame her. It's not *that* good of a school. But I didn't want to be saddled with hundreds of thousands of dollars of debt. I've currently paid off $5,000 of the $15,000 I owe. Judie, of course, owes nothing. Kelly probably got an art scholarship or something, knowing her.

I spend my Saturday morning sitting on my bed with my laptop in front of me, and a nice big mug of coffee on my bedside table. I'm kind of craving some barbecue nachos, but something about eating them at 9:30 in the morning grosses me out.

On my laptop, I open up a new blank Google Doc and start outlining my article. I'm not sure of everything I'm going to say yet, and I'm still not sure how to make mine stand apart from Alice Gilbert's.

Then it hits me. I can talk about my sister.

I outline what parts of Judie's experiences, and my conflict with her, I want to disclose to the entire internet, trying my best to imagine what she'd be okay with me telling the entire world. I'm not going to be all that limited. In case you haven't noticed, Judie's comfort zone is huge. Plus, she'll probably be ecstatic to have "flattering" pictures of her new body out there for everyone to see. I make a mental note to ask her later about doing a photoshoot.

As I'm free-writing some general ideas for the article, Judie bursts through my door, looking like she's about to go to a nightclub. She's dressed in a skirt barely long enough to cover her full butt (especially her *new* butt, which is huge), and a crop top that shows off her flat stomach and bountiful cleavage.

"You're aware it's not even ten in the morning yet, right?" I ask her, glancing up from my laptop screen.

"I'm going to brunch!" she announces.

"That's what you wear to *brunch*?"

She nods. "Michelle and Mikayla and I are meeting up with some guys we met last night at the bar. We're getting unlimited mimosas!"

It's times like these that I sometimes doubt that Judie and I have any kind of sister mind-connection because the thought of *binge* drinking in the morning has never even crossed my mind.

"Well," I say, trying to be as encouraging as I can, "I hope this new guy's better than the last two."

"His name is Pierre," she says. "He's from France. I'm gonna get him to buy me French toast."

"You realize French toast isn't *actually* French, right?"

Judie rolls her eyes at me. "Of *course*, I know that, Amber. It's a pun. Sometimes you think I'm so stupid."

"Sorry." I smile at her. "Have fun with your Frenchman."

"Have fun with your laptop," she says.

"Actually, I'm going out with Kelly later."

"Oh, cool! Then I'll have fun with my Frenchman, and you'll have fun with your...what nationality *is* Kelly anyway?"

I shrug. "I dunno. American, I'm assuming."

"Yeah, but I mean, like where's her family from?"

"Like her ancestors? How should I know? I don't even know where *our* ancestors are from."

"I think Mom once said we're part German."

"Judie, be honest with me. Did you pregame brunch?"

"Only a little," she says, giggling. "I had *one* glass of white wine."

"Go to brunch, Judie."

Then she leaves.

At noon, I meet Kelly for lunch at Crunchy's Diner. I get my usual, The Amber, and she gets a salad with sprouts and beans and stuff. I didn't even know Crunchy's *had* food that healthy. But leave it to Kelly to find it.

"I'm excited to see your college campus," she says.

"Me too."

"You're excited to see your own college campus, too?"

"I meant that I'm excited to *show* it to you. But if I'm being totally honest, it would be nice to see it while in daylight and completely sober. There are some gaps in my memories."

Kelly laughs and takes a sip of her coffee.

I finish my burger, and we head out. I show Kelly the dorm building I lived in freshman and sophomore year, before Brianne and I got an apartment together. I show her the alleyways between buildings where Brianne and I used to smoke weed sophomore year so we wouldn't get in trouble in the dorms.

"How much weed did you smoke in college?" she asks.

"I mean, a decent amount. I wasn't like, a total stoner. Just on weekends. How about you? I'm guessing none since you're, like, the healthiest person I've ever met."

She shrugs. "I tried it with Zack a few times. But I didn't like it that much. I'm not opposed to it or anything, though."

For some reason, I still get a little nauseous when she mentions Zack. I brush it off, and we continue our tour of the campus.

"Ooh! Here, I know somewhere you'd like." I grab her hand and pull her toward the art building.

My plan is to take Kelly through the art building and see if there are any student paintings or sculptures on display.

But before we can even get inside the building, Kelly's attention is already captured.

"Woah! Look at this!" she runs toward an outdoor student art display on the steps leading to the building's entrance.

Three students are standing across the steps, blocking off the door. They've all clearly taken insane doses of Lipamorph, and have altered their bodies into surrealist sculptures.

The three girls stand there, still as statues, wearing nothing but thin black underwear and duct tape X's over their nipples.

The girl on the left has a giant left boob, as big as her head, and no right boob at all. She also has a massive right thigh, and a left thigh so thin that her round kneecap looks like it's about to bulge out of her skin. In the middle stands a girl who has moved most of her body fat to her face, so much that she looks like a bobblehead. She's also moved some weight to her calves and feet, which I'm assuming is so she doesn't fall over. On the far right, the girl has moved a bunch of fat to her hands and feet, so that they bulge out like a cartoon character.

It's creepy, disgusting, and fascinating all the same.

I glance over at Kelly, who stares at the display, her eyes transfixed. "Just a second," she whispers to me. Then she struts up to the students on the stairs.

"Hey," she asks them. "Do you mind if I take a picture of you guys? I kind of want to draw this when I get home."

"Go ahead," says the bobblehead in the middle.

Kelly takes her phone out of her back pocket and snaps a few pictures of them. Then she puts a ten-dollar bill in their donation jar.

The whole walk back to the "L" Kelly keeps muttering things like, "Wow. That was so cool. That was just the coolest thing," under her breath.

20

KELLY

Amber sits cross-legged on my green armchair with Sienna curled up in her lap, while I sit on the floor in front of her, leaning my sketchbook up against the chair's base.

"Have I shown you my anatomy studies?" I ask her.

"Not yet, no. I've only seen the art on your walls, for the most part."

I open up to a page in my sketchbook, where I drew Jessica from page 14 of *Playboy*.

"That's really good," Amber says. "Not that I'm surprised, or anything. You're, like, an art prodigy or something."

I think about telling her that, in order to be a prodigy, you had to excel as a child, and my art was only mediocre when I was a kid. I got better through all the practicing I did as a teenager. But instead, I just keep talking about anatomy studies.

"That display at your college was amazing," I tell her. "I feel like I need to make some kind of new piece based on what they were doing. But I'm not sure what yet. But at least for sketching purposes, they'd be great for, like, *anti*-anatomy studies."

Amber nods along. "That sounds cool. Like a statement about how Lipamorph is turning women into nothing but works of art on display for us to look at. Or something."

I'm still not sure how to tell Amber that I'm not actually opposed to Lipamorph, so I just nod. Amber can be feisty as hell—it's one of the things I love about her—but I'm not sure I'm ready to take her on in a full-blown argument just yet.

After I turn to a blank page in my sketchbook, I look up at Amber, who looks so peaceful stroking Sienna's fur. And then I get an idea.

"Hey, can I draw *you*?"

Amber shrugs. "Yeah, sure, of course. If you want to. I'm not sure I'm that interesting of a subject."

"Well, *I* think you're pretty."

Amber chuckles. "Nobody thinks I'm pretty. You're just trying to get me into bed."

"I can get you into bed whenever I want. Plus, I know you well enough by now to know that you don't even care about being *pretty* that much because you hate the way society reduces women to their appearance. So if I were trying to impress you, do you really think that's the compliment I'd go for?"

Amber just bursts out laughing at that. "You really *do* know me, Kelly from Marketing."

"I know I do. Now hold still. I'm going to draw you with Sienna in your lap."

"I'll hold still," she says. "But I can't be held responsible for anything the cat does."

About ten minutes pass, and I'm finishing up the outline of the picture—the chair, Amber's body, and Sienna in her lap.

"So do I just sit here silently, or can I talk?" she asks. "Or will my talking distract you?"

"No, go ahead. Talk away. Just don't change your body position."

"Hmm, okay." She glances up toward the ceiling, looking thoughtful. "What do you want to talk about?"

I start blocking out the proportions of her face. "Tell me about your family."

"Okay. Well, you already know Judie. That's about all there is to know."

"What about your parents?" I start adding the details to her eyes.

"Judie and I don't talk to them. They don't really like us all that much."

I glance up at Amber. For the first time since I've met her, her eyes actually look sad. Or maybe that's because I'm just focusing on her eyes more than I ever have before. You know, for the picture.

"I'm really sorry to hear that."

She shrugs. Then laughs. "Sorry. I won't shrug anymore. Don't want to mess up your picture."

I wave her concerns away with my left hand, continuing to draw with my right.

She continues talking. "Judie and I kind of had a falling out with our parents my senior year of high school, when I was eighteen and she was sixteen. My parents, they're... traditionalists, I guess I'd call them. I guess that's the politically correct way to put it."

I just nod, indicating for her to go on.

"Well, that year, we were both just huge disappointments to them. Me because I went to prom with another girl. I mean, I'd already tried to tell them I was gay a few times, but they pretended not to listen, I think. Then since Judie and I were both going to prom that year, they got so excited to get pictures of both of their daughters together, but then when I brought my female date home, they got all upset."

"That sucks." I shake my head, not looking up from my drawing. "What about Judie? What was her problem with them?"

"Well, at first, they were mad because she took my side. But, um...it was actually a bigger deal for her. Because at the end of that school year, right before I went off to college, Judie was...well, you know, uh...she got pregnant."

I have to stop drawing for a second to look up at Amber. "Oh God."

"Yeah," she nods a little. "We don't talk about it much anymore since it was such a rough time. She ended up miscarrying after two months, so it was okay. We didn't need to make any big decisions. But our parents, they found the pregnancy test in the trash, and they were pretty sure it didn't come from the daughter that constantly tried to tell them she only likes women."

"So what happened?"

"I mean, we just kind of cut ourselves off from them. Judie and I defended each other through it all. They took care of her until she graduated high school, of course, but then she moved into a small place with her friends Michelle and Mikayla while working at Big Mama's Coffee. Then she moved in with me after I graduated college. That's about it. We were just both huge disappointments to them."

"God, I'm so sorry, Amber." I shake my head, looking up at her. This time, not just to study her for my drawing, but to make sure she's okay. "That's awful."

"It's okay," she says. "I just...I feel really worried for Judie sometimes. She's always had a really tough time with her body. All throughout high school, she kept trying to prove her worth with guys. And don't get me wrong, I didn't have any problem with her dating guys. But they definitely took advantage of her insecurity. And now that she has this perfect body, I see it happening to her even more. I just don't know what to do."

I honestly have no idea what to say to that. So I just nod and keep drawing.

"How about you?" she asks. "Tell me about your family. They're probably better than mine, at least."

I shake my head. "I mean, they're okay. They mean well overall. They're always disappointed in whoever I decide to date, though."

"So I guess they're not going to be meeting me anytime soon, then?" she asks with a smile.

"I don't know. It's not *you*. My mom didn't like Zack either. Even after I dated him for three years."

"Why not? What was wrong with Zack?"

"Nothing. She just wants me to date a Korean man."

"What?! That is the most random thing I've ever heard."

I shake my head, laughing a little. I outline a smile on Amber's face. "It's not, really. My mom is Korean, and my dad's Irish, and she always says that marrying a non-Korean man was the biggest mistake she ever made. They've been divorced since I was four."

"Wow. I'm sorry to hear that."

"No, it's okay. Life's not about impressing other people." I'm not sure how much I really mean that, but it sounds meaningful in the moment.

"It couldn't have been that big of a mistake," Amber says, scratching Sienna behind the ears. "Because you resulted from it, right?"

"I guess so." I smile. Then, I add Amber's freckles.

21

JUDIE

MONDAY AT BIG MAMA'S, I'M LOST IN THOUGHT, thinking about Pierre. Not in a dreamy way. In a frustrated way.

Why. Do. Men. Suck??

I would ask Amber, but it would be the biggest I-told-you-so moment of her life. And maybe we'd get into another fight like we did the last time I told her I hated men.

For the record, I didn't mean to accuse her of victim blaming. Even though she kind of was. I just don't like it when she judges my life choices so harshly. But then, I wonder, what if she's right? What if I should just go back to my regular body? The one I hated?

Pierre tried to feel me up at *the breakfast table*. In a *public restaurant*. And he kept speaking to me in French. I think he had some weird misconception that American girls find it romantic when guys speak to them in French. But I just found it annoying. I couldn't understand a word the guy was saying! So, of course, that just made me trust him even less.

I ended up leaving brunch before Michelle and Mikayla even finished their pancakes.

So today, I'm just leaning against the counter, resting my head in my right hand and pondering all of this. Our morning rush is over, so there isn't all that much to do right now anyway.

"Got your head in the clouds again, Stiles?" Luke asks, barging in from the back room. He's carrying a giant bottle of dish soap and a clean rag. "I know there are no customers, but we could get ahead on cleaning some of the dishes from this morning."

I stand up straight and turn around to face him. "Yeah, we *could*, I guess." I glance over at the rack of clean mugs on the wall. We definitely have enough to get through the rest of the day. "But the real question is, *should* we?"

Luke laughs at that, and leans against the counter next to me. "We don't have to right now. But we *do* need to get this place sparkling clean for the first of next month."

"What's happening on the first of the month?"

He gets a big smile on his face, like he's got an awesome surprise he's about to reveal. "My mom's coming for a visit. She's planning to stay for all of November."

"*The* Big Mama?!"

"The one and only!"

That officially makes me smile. Luke's mother founded Big Mama's Coffee twenty years ago, when Luke was a little boy. Little eight-year-old Luke would help out around the kitchen, washing and drying dishes, and sometimes even greeting customers. She named it Big Mama's because she wanted to emphasize that she was a mom first and a coffee shop owner second. I guess that's where Luke's adorably ambiguous child labor came in. Still, I've heard plenty of stories about Luke's mom, that I'm *super* excited to finally meet her.

"I'm assuming I shouldn't call her Big Mama," I say with a laugh. "What's her actual name?"

Luke shrugs. "You can call her Big Mama if you want. She likes that, actually. But her name is Paulina."

"Paulina Loughner. Sounds nice."

Luke shakes his head at that. "No, she's not a Loughner. She changed her last name back to Papadopoulos after she and my dad got divorced."

"Sorry to hear that."

He waves my apology away with his hand. "Don't be. They got divorced when I was three, before this coffee shop was even a twinkle in my mom's eye."

"Paulina Papadopoulos and Luke Loughner. Sounds like a great management team."

"We were."

Luke and I just stand there in silence for a moment. Then, he finally breaks it. "So, if you don't want to clean, what *do* you want to do while there are no customers here?"

"I don't know."

"Just brood all day?"

"Brood?" I didn't know that my sadness had been all that obvious. Amber always says I'm shitty at hiding my emotions. She's probably right; she's usually pretty perceptive.

"I can tell something's upsetting you. I'm used to Judie Stiles strutting into work every morning like a model on a runway, ready to kick the world's ass one latte at a time."

I smile at that. Luke's got a real talent for making me laugh, even if it's just internally.

"These past few days, though," he continues, "It's like something's sucked the life out of you."

Part of me wants to tell Luke everything because he's a sweet and funny guy, and I know he'll know exactly how to make me feel better. The other part of me, though, doesn't want Luke to know I've been going on so many dates. I still like Luke and have always wanted there to be a possibility of us ending up together. I just never felt comfortable making a move on my *boss*. It always felt inappropriate. But I don't want him to think I'm *not* interested in him, either.

So instead, I just say the first thing that comes to my head, which I'm not sure is a good idea. "Have you noticed my new body?"

He nods. "Of course I have. You can't miss it."

"Guys really like my new body."

He chuckles at that. "I'm not surprised. What are you trying to say, Judie? Is someone harassing you or something? Is that why you've been so—"

I shake my head. "No, it's not like *that*. It's like...I guess lately, I feel like people *only* like me for my body. I'm just conflicted, I guess. Because I *like* looking this way, but then at the same time, I don't because I feel like people are putting my appearance before *me*."

"That sucks," Luke says, nodding. "I guess I've never

had to deal with anything like that. My body's nothing to write home about." He pats his large tummy.

I want to tell him that I *like* his body and that I *have* written home about it. Well, not literally written home. Just talked about it at home with Amber. But I'm worried I'll sound like I'm hitting on my boss. Which, if I said those things, I *would* be doing, so the worry is valid.

"Judie," he continues. "You *should* look the way that makes you most happy. And if anyone gives you shit for that, well...you just let me know who I need to beat up."

I laugh at that. "I will." That's a partial lie since I've already decided not to tell him about Pierre, Josh, and Ken. Maybe I will one day but not today.

"Hey, where's the music? Aren't you always blasting that Mrs. Candybar?"

"Miz Lollipop?"

"Yeah, that's the one! Why's it so *quiet* here today?"

I guess that, in my "brooding," as Luke would call it, I forgot to put the music on. So I hook my phone up to the speaker and "Worship Dat Booty" begins.

"That's more like it!" he says, throwing his hands in the air. "Until the next customer comes in, we're going to have a dance party!"

Like I said, Luke *always* knows how to cheer me up.

So we start dancing all around the coffee shop. Behind the counter, around the couches, everywhere. When Miz Lollipop reaches the second chorus, Luke grabs my hand and spins me in a circle. Once I've spun fully around, and I'm facing him again, he pulls me in toward his body. And then, just like that, out of nowhere, we kiss.

At first I think it's just going to be a quick thing, but then it keeps going. And going and going and going, and I realize I don't want it to stop.

And then, stupid Greta comes in to order a pumpkin spice.

22

AMBER

Perfect

By Amber Stiles

What makes something a drug?

MY SISTER—WHO HATES DRUGS—SAYS IT HAS TO HURT your body in some way or alter your perception of the world. If you can't get high off of it, it's not a drug.

What counts as "getting high"? My sister takes Lipamorph pills like they're candy. She doesn't think she's getting high, even though she's high off of the confidence that comes with having a perfect body.

What makes someone "perfect"? I guess that's the real question today.

I'm skinny. Some people would say my body is perfect. Most wouldn't though because skinny is ALL I am. Most wouldn't see perfection in the way my jeans hang off my hips or the way my lack of boobs is so easily hidden under a sweatshirt.

Who determines what "perfect" is?

In "Loathing Lipamorph," Alice Gilbert's Feminist Forum article from last month, she argues that perfection is defined by men and that the beauty standards imposed on women result from a patriarchal society. I would agree with her.

Men have always unfairly treated my sister like a sex object, from the gross, immature boys in high school to the guys she meets at bars with her friends six years later. Now that her body is what men would call "perfect," they've gone beyond treating her like an object to treating her like a prize. My beautiful sister, who is now, by most men's standards, "perfect," should have that power to hold over them. But instead, she's played into their hand, and they're ready to take full advantage.

In the interest of being direct, I do not support Lipamorph. Like everything in life, I support a woman's right to make her own choice on what to do with her body, so I do support the legality of Lipamorph. But I don't support the cultural acceptance of it.

I don't support the way it's marketed solely at women. I've never once seen a Lipamorph ad featuring a man wanting to change his body. Maybe one day, when a new drug allows you to change your muscle definition or something, I'll be writing something different. (Probably not, though, because if the drug were to change muscle definition, it would change our perceptions of a man's strength—not of his fertility.) No one has even acted like Lipamorph could be something men would consider using. All of the spokespeople are female celebrities. Why is this?

Most likely because men are born knowing they're "perfect." They're told to focus on their education, their strength, their leadership. Appearance is an afterthought.

Just a few days ago, my sister started dating a wonderful guy who likes her for who she is, not just her body. He's a little chubby himself and has always had a sense of humor about it.

She asked him if men ever use Lipamorph. He just said, "Oh. I've never thought about it. It's kind of like makeup I guess...something men could use, but I'm not really sure why they'd feel the need to."

I'm glad my sister has finally found someone who supports her personal decisions with her body and cares about more than her appearance.

At the same time, I hate that she—and countless other women I see on TV, on the bus, on the streets, and in my own office building—feel the need to chemically alter themselves to be accepted. I hate that it's so mainstream.

I hate that, no matter what year it is, no matter how far we as a society have progressed, women will always bear the burden of needing to look perfect.

Submitted October 4 to feministforum.com.
Status: Pending publication.

23

KELLY

Rebecca finally picks a book.

There's no discussion, no debate, nothing. She just barges into Amber and Samantha's basement office for our meeting on Friday and throws a stack of books into the air.

"We're reading *Brian's Song*!" she announces, as paperback copies hit the floor around us.

"Did you buy us all copies, or did you just have eight copies of *Brian's Song* sitting in your house?" Midge asks with a laugh.

Rebecca rolls her eyes. "I don't have *eight* copies. I had to buy two of them."

I actually knew this about Rebecca already. She once told me that back in high school, she and a bunch of her friends put on an all-female production of *Brian's Song* at a youth theater festival. She didn't *intend* for it to be an all-female production, in the sense that she wasn't trying to make any kind of statement about the lack of women in football or anything. She just really, *really* likes *Brian's Song* and wanted to direct a play about Chicago. They did not win. I once asked her why she didn't put on *Chicago* instead since that play actually *is* female-focused. She just ruffled my hair, called me "New York trash," and mentioned that nobody *in* Chicago actually likes the musical *Chicago.* (I don't think that's true.) That and she can't sing. (I do believe that part.)

I'm not at all surprised she kept six copies of the *Brian's Song* script all these years.

"Is this even really a book?" Midge asks, flipping through it. "It's a script. Like, for a movie."

Rebecca nods. "Yeah, but we've had this club for, like, a month and no one else has chosen a book. And, as I mentioned, I already had six copies of this one."

So that's that. We're reading *Brian's Song.* Nobody has any better book suggestions anyway. I'm actually kind of surprised that Rebecca didn't already make me read this—or at least watch the movie—as part of the hardcore Chicago initiation she gave me back when I first moved here.

"So, we'll discuss this next week," says Rebecca. "Then I'm putting one of you guys in charge of picking the next book. Any volunteers?"

We all glance at each other. Rebecca looks right at me. "Hey," I say, "I already suggested *Harry Potter* at the first meeting, and no one was into it."

"That's because most of us have already read it," says Isabelle.

Isabelle's voice has been sounding more professional lately. Like she's talking more and squeaking less. Like, there isn't an *actual* change. It has the same pitch and everything. She just sounds more sure of herself. I like it.

"How about you pick the next one?" I ask her.

"Okay," she says. "I'll look through my shelves. I hope you guys like young-adult romance."

"*Love* it," says Tanya, at the same time as Amber says, "Not really."

Oh well. I don't really like based-on-a-true-story sports plots, but here we are. I'm kind of excited to see what Isabelle brings in.

"Great," says Rebecca. "So Isabelle, how about you bring in the next book in three weeks? That'll give us some time to finish this one."

Isabelle nods.

"So," Rebecca continues, "should we assign parts and read this like a play, or should we just read the first half at home over the week?"

"Read at home," a bunch of us say in unison.

Rebecca looks mildly disappointed. I think she wanted a chance to reprise her glory-days role as Chicago football hero Brian Piccolo. But none of the rest of us really want to act, let alone pretend to be men.

We sit in awkward silence for a few moments, while Rebecca flips through the book and makes little notes in it with her blue pen, probably trying to find discussion points for next week's meeting.

While Rebecca's busy, Fanny Spitzer turns to Tanya. "I was thinking about what you mentioned last week," says Fanny. "About Lipamorph being just another way women have choice over their bodies."

"What about it?" asks Tanya.

"Well, I was wondering, what do you think about children using it?"

"I'm not sure," Tanya says. "I mean, on the one hand, young girls should have choice over their bodies, too. But on the other hand, it's only been approved for women over eighteen, so I'm not sure it would be safe. I'm not really sure."

Fanny nods. "I'm concerned about my daughter," she says. "I think she wants to try it."

"Maybe just provide a safe environment for her to try it in, then. And monitor how much she uses," Tanya suggests.

Fanny shakes her head. "I'm not comfortable with that. She's too young to be making her body look so...so sexualized. And I'm not okay with a thirteen-year-old girl using a drug underage."

"My cousin uses it and she's sixteen," Samantha cuts in.

We all turn to look at Samantha. Even though this was previously a conversation between just Fanny and Tanya, suddenly we're all engaged. I guess the fact that Samantha talks so rarely makes us really *listen* when she finally does speak up.

"What do you think about your cousin using it so young?" asks Fanny.

"I support it. She's transgender and just started hormone therapy like a year ago, so she's still working on trying to get a body that's...I guess, feminine looking, for lack of a better word."

I really appreciate that Samantha brought this point up.

But I don't say anything. I always feel weird speaking up when our group fights about Lipamorph. Probably because I know one day, it's going to lead to a fight between me and Amber, and I'm not sure I'm ready for that yet. Things have been really good between us, and I'm just not great with conflict.

"I thought you were on *our* side, Samantha," says Fanny. "Wasn't it you who, last week, said Lipamorph was turning the perfect feminine body from an *ideal* to an *expectation*?"

Samantha shakes her head. "It's not about taking sides. And I still believe what I said last week. But I think it's important for it still to *exist* for people like my cousin who need it. I guess I'm just saying that it's not as black and white of an issue as we want to make it."

Samantha should talk more. Whenever she does, she always manages to say these reasonable, level-headed things that diffuse a fight in an instant. Samantha should run for fucking president. But she's probably going to be the next Bill Gates or something instead.

After the meeting adjourns, I still have ten minutes before I have to return to Finnegan & Peters from my lunch break, so I follow Amber into the basement bathroom.

Like usual, we're making out in the stall farthest from the sink. But something's different today. She's not as into it. She seems hesitant, like her head's in the clouds. Amber's never struck me as a head-in-the-clouds type, so I pull back for a second.

"Everything okay?"

She nods. "Yeah, mostly. It's just...I appreciate what

Samantha said today. And like...I guess I just wish I'd taken that kind of thing into account before I'd written my article."

"Article?"

"I thought I told you. I just wrote a new post for *The Feminist Forum*."

I nod. "I think you mentioned it, but you didn't say what it was about. It was, like, an in-passing thing." By in-passing, I mean that she mentioned it yesterday while we were coming up for air in between bathroom kisses.

"Oh, sorry. It's about Lipamorph. And basically what Samantha said last week, about how it takes female perfection from an ideal to an expectation. And how we need to stop pressuring women to be perfect when we don't put the same pressure on men. But I didn't realize that I just totally glossed over the whole population of people who are in the process of becoming biologically female."

I nod. I think that's when I realize that, one day, we *are* going to have to fight about this. About Lipamorph and what it means for a woman to alter her body. And I just hope that when that day comes, things stay really good between us.

But that day is not today. So I just nod and kiss her again.

24

JUDIE

Luke and I have been dating for a week now, and it's been the best week of my life! We've even hung out with Amber. And *she* even enjoyed it!

Since we kissed on Monday, Luke and I have been hanging out outside of our shifts at Big Mama's. Even though I get off of work by six most days of the week and Luke has to stay until nine to close up the shop, he's still come over to my apartment almost every night. A few times, we've watched some sitcoms with Amber and played one of her drinking games.

Luke named our sitcom drinking game "Shitcoms." Because we're drinking to shitty sitcoms. And, get this! Amber found that funny! Maybe it's not that shocking. But in my twenty-two years as Amber's sister, I've never once seen her smile at anything a member of the male species has said or done. Partially because she's always been so protective of me. But now that she doesn't feel I need protecting anymore and she's finally found a male person she approves of, it's refreshing.

Still, there's been a nagging thought at the back of my head all week.

What if Luke's really just mostly into my body, too?

Okay, I know it doesn't sound all that logical on the surface, right? Because Luke hasn't even *tried* to have sex with me yet. Sure, we've made out a bunch in Big Mama's stock room when there have been no customers in the café. And sure, he regularly compliments how nice I look when I come to work each day. But his conversations with me never feel like thinly veiled pick-up lines. It feels like he's really interested in dancing to pop music and making fun of sitcoms and, of course, making lattes with me.

Yet, for some reason, the feeling persists. Maybe it's because Luke never made any kind of move until after I got this new body. And, to be fair, I didn't make a move on him either, but it's because I was worried about him being my boss. But he clearly had no problem with that issue the entire time. So, why did he wait until now? Was it the new body? Did he not find me attractive before?

Of course, leave it to Luke to know when there's something on my mind. I can't hide anything from this guy.

"Okay, what's wrong this time, Stiles?" he asks from the sink in the back. He's washing out dirty mugs, while I stare into space at the cash register.

I could just say, "Nothing, it's okay, don't worry," but I don't want to be dishonest with him. Plus, the last time I was honest with Luke about what was wrong, we ended up kissing. And starting a relationship.

So, instead, I say, "Why did you wait so long to make your move?"

He shrugs and laughs quietly to himself. "I don't know. Why did *you*?"

"Well, you were my boss. And I wasn't sure if it would be appropriate."

He puts a dried mug back on the shelf and comes to stand next to me at the counter. "I don't know if you've noticed," he says, "but Big Mama's Coffee isn't exactly known for our hyper-professionalism."

"That's fair," I answer with a laugh. "But I guess, I mean...why did you wait to make a move until *after* I changed my body? I mean, I guess I'm just wondering, like... did you suddenly become attracted to me when I got a better body?"

"Aw, Judie," he laughs softly again, but I can tell something in his eyes looks guilty. "Okay, first of all, 'better' is relative, especially when it comes to someone's body. Your old body looked much more like mine. So it couldn't have been *all* that bad."

I laugh a little at that. He's right. His body *definitely* isn't all bad, even if he is a little chubby.

"But I see what you're saying," he continues. "Here's what I think. When you first changed your body, you seemed more confident. You seemed happier with the way you looked. And I guess, by proxy, that made me happy with the way you looked. So I think it was the additional confidence I was attracted to. Does that make sense?"

I nod. "It does."

"I love your body. But I'd love your body if you decided to go back to the way it was before, too. I just want you to be happy."

Sometimes, I think Luke is too good for this world. Or at least for a small one-location coffee shop on the North Side of Chicago.

"Hold on a second," he says, ducking into the storage room. He comes out a second later with an envelope in his hand. "I was going to wait until the end of our shift to give this to you, but you needed some cheering up now. So here. I got you an early birthday gift."

A small laugh escapes as my eyebrows furrow. "But my birthday isn't for four months."

"I know when your birthday is, Stiles," he says, handing me the small white envelope. "But this is a time-sensitive gift, so you're getting it four months early."

I rip it open, and when I see what's inside, I actually gasp out loud.

"Miz Lollipop!"

"Yep." He nods, smiling. "I know how much you like her, and I must admit, after hearing you play her music so much at work, you've turned me into a fan. So we're gonna see her."

Miz Lollipop and Betty J are about to embark on their yearly U.S. tour, and they're stopping in Chicago this December. I'd been looking at tickets online here and there but didn't think I'd be able to afford any of them and still make rent. Most of the cheap seats were sold out months ago, and only the tickets worth $100 and up were left. Luke must've spent a fortune.

"I don't even know how to thank you for this," I say, worrying I'm about to start stuttering or something. "This is so great. Thank you so much!"

Then I leap onto him for a hug, and he catches my waist in his arms.

25

AMBER

It's Saturday, and I'm on a double date.

This is the first time in my life I've *ever* been on a double date. I thought they were a high school thing, honestly. But I guess adult couples get together to hang out in sitcoms all the time. So maybe not. If Monica and Chandler can spend all day at the Central Perk with Ross and Rachel, why can't we?

Because this is still *me* we're talking about, the double date consists of me, Kelly, Judie, and Luke all crammed into our living room, marathoning *According to Jim* and drinking rum and Coke. One of the local Chicago channels regularly shows *According to Jim* reruns. I guess because it takes place here. They're also quite fond of *Mike and Molly*.

I've also made some hors d'oeuvres specifically for the occasion. By hors d'oeuvres, I mean barbecue nachos and off-brand Fritos drizzled in hot buffalo sauce.

At first, Kelly took one look at my hors d'oeuvres and asked, "Is this going to be like The Amber from Crunchy's?"

But, of course, I made her try them anyway. And I learned that Kelly actually *likes* barbecue nachos! Which are just tortilla chips with melted Colby Jack, covered in a thick layer of Sweet Baby Ray's barbecue sauce. No barbecued meat or anything, so they're Kelly-friendly.

Judie and I have been talking for a while about getting Netflix, or some other kind of streaming service, because it's getting really annoying having to sit through commercials during our sitcom marathons. The only reason we haven't yet is that the cable comes free with our internet service, and we didn't want to pay any extra monthly fees. That's like ten dollars a month I could be spending on more controversial burgers for Kelly.

But what happens today takes the cake.

The news people actually *interrupt* our *According to Jim* marathon.

When the news cuts off one of Jim and Cheryl's signature arguments, I throw a chip at the TV. Don't worry. I'd already sucked all the barbecue sauce off of it, so I didn't ruin the screen.

"John Belushi's rolling over in his grave right now!" I yell at the screen, half-drunk.

"That's Jim Belushi, his brother, in this show," says Kelly. "He's still alive."

I guess when I'm drunk, Kelly knows more about sitcoms than I do. Still, I don't want to watch the *news* right now.

"A protest has broken out in downtown Chicago, near City Hall," says the conventionally perfect-looking blonde news anchor.

I guess that's one of the downsides to watching a

marathon that airs only on a local Chicago channel. Every single thing that happens in Chicago is breaking news.

"Can someone go find a streaming site?" I ask. "Project Free TV or something?"

"Let me see if I can find my Netflix password," Kelly says, scrolling through the Notes app on her phone. Of course Kelly has Netflix. I'm briefly thankful that we've never watched it together—we must still be in the more interesting, getting-to-know-you phase of our relationship before we fall into the Netflix-on-the-couch phase.

"Wait!" says Judie. "Leave it on the news for a sec."

Apparently, the protest outside of City Hall is over Lipamorph. It's not just Chicago, either. They're breaking out all over the place because of a new bill that's going through Congress.

The news cuts to Dr. John Kelso, MD, whose name is displayed in a title strip across the bottom of the screen. "Since the release of Lipamorph, we've seen a 20% increase in the obesity rate among women," he explains. "That's *huge*." I'm assuming the pun is unintended. "This stuff's only been available for a couple months, and already, people are using it as a crutch, so that they can eat whatever they want with no consequences." The obesity rate is *always* increasing, so I'm not sure what exactly Dr. John Kelso, MD is on about. Targeting a drug that primarily women use and declaring it the cause without further research is pretty sexist. And regardless of whether or not I support Lipamorph itself, I do not support Dr. John Kelso, MD, or any other men who try to tell women what's best for them.

When it cuts back to Conventionally Attractive Blonde Anchor (henceforth referred to as CABA), we learn more about the debate going on. "Local politicians in many cities throughout the US, including right here in Chicago, are proposing bills to regulate the usage of Lipamorph, to prevent a national health decline."

"That bitch is hypocritical as hell," Judie half-drunkenly mumbles.

"What do you mean?" I ask.

"She wouldn't have gotten that job if she didn't look as good as she does. You ever seen an ugly news anchor?"

"A few," Kelly cuts in. "But they're all men."

"Exactly," says Judie.

As time goes on, I'm starting to see Judie's point more and more. And also starting to regret the article I submitted to *The Feminist Forum*. I'm starting to wonder if I should email an editor there and ask them to pull it from their publication queue.

But at the same time, I don't want to. Because what Judie's saying is true; that anchor probably *wouldn't* have gotten that job if she didn't look "perfect." And if *all* women are starting to look "perfect," will there even be any jobs left for those of us who don't? For those of us who don't *want* to take the pills? Or maybe people who *can't* because it reacts with another medicine or something?

It's like Samantha said; none of this is as black and white as we want it to be.

After some quick interviews with protesters in the crowd—all saying things about the need to protect our freedom to do whatever we want with our bodies, without government intervention, and that women can be trusted to manage their own health, thank you very much—Dr. John Kelso, MD comes back on screen. "We've especially been worried about the health complications in the wake of what's recently happened to Miz Lollipop, just earlier today—"

"Hold the fuck up!" Judie screams, throwing herself off the couch and landing on the floor in front of the TV. She lands directly on her boobs, which are proving once again to be a useful cushion. "What happened to Miz Lollipop?!"

Judie's lying on her stomach on the floor, glancing between the TV screen and her cell phone, where she scrolls through #MizLollipop on Twitter and tries to piece together the story. She doesn't need to wait long because, as it turns out, that's the next part of the news story.

As it turns out, Lipamorph has an unintended side effect that no one knew about, I guess because no one had used it for long enough yet to find out. But, at least according to CABA, Miz Lollipop had been abusing Lipamorph for *years*, long before any of us common people even knew about it. So had Betty J and Ella Esmeralda, I guess, but they had yet to overdose.

Apparently, when Miz Lollipop overdosed on Lipamorph this morning, she lost control of the fat in her body, and suddenly the fat could go wherever it wanted without warning. So somehow, this morning 93% of the fat in her body moved to her left arm.

"Exclusive" (invasive) footage flashes across the screen of

Miz Lollipop in the hospital: her left arm a spherical blob covered in an array of stretch marks, skin turning a dark purple shade from a lack of circulation. The rest of her body is skin and bones; elbows, knees, ribs, and hips looking ready to puncture her tight skin.

A voice-over tells us about the hospital's plans to amputate Miz Lollipop's left arm, then pump additional fat into the rest of her body.

Kelly's face flushes, and she quickly makes a run for the bathroom. A few seconds later, we hear the sound of her vomit splattering in the toilet.

Judie looks horrified. I don't know if it's because she's worried for Miz Lollipop or worried for herself. Maybe a little of both.

I'm about to slide off the couch and go sit next to Judie, so I can pat her shoulder and tell her it's going to be okay, but Luke actually beats me to it.

Luke is the first boyfriend of Judie's I've actually liked.

So instead, I head to the bathroom to check on Kelly.

26

KELLY

The following week at work, Amber and I plan a bunch of dates to go on. Things continue to go perfectly between us. Honestly, it's a relief to me. I was *really* worried she was going to be grossed out by me after she heard me vomiting at her house on Saturday.

But she wasn't. She just came into the bathroom, asked me if I was okay, and then held my hair back for me. Then she gave me a hug and got me some water. I thanked her for not being grossed out.

She just laughed. "Nothing grosses me out. See Exhibit A: The Amber on the Crunchy's menu."

That made me laugh, too. She even kissed me. On the mouth. After I vomited. Before I even had a chance to brush my teeth or anything. I remember thinking to myself, *Amber's a keeper*.

That's why this week, we're having all kinds of fun dates together.

On Monday, we have lunch together in Millennium Park, on the grass. On Tuesday, we leave each other notes in the basement bathroom that nobody else uses. She sticks

Post-It notes on the back of the door inside the stall farthest from the sink, and I tape white index cards underneath them.

Hey Kelly! Enjoy your pee! Love, Amber

Hi Amber! Don't spend too long in the bathroom. You might miss a call from someone who forgot how to use a mouse or a keyboard. Love, Kelly

Hi there, Kelly from Marketing! Don't you spend too long in the bathroom, either, or else you'll fall asleep on the toilet, and Midge will have to drag you out again. Love, Amber

Amber!!! You need to let that go!!! Still love you. Kelly

On Wednesday, we have dinner together in an abandoned "L" stop.

Amber takes me to the Monroe Red Line stop, which is one of the underground subway stops. From the Monroe stop, you can walk straight along the platform north to the Lake stop or south to the Jackson stop. It's a decently long walk in between each stop, so most people don't do it. And in between each stop is either dead space or abandoned train stops from the past.

I'll have to reprimand Rebecca for never showing me this.

It's rush hour right now, meaning the subway platforms are crowded with people waiting to squeeze like sardines into a train car. Amber's wearing a grey backpack, which she filled with dinner for us. It's the closest thing either of us have to a picnic basket, and Amber promised me she wouldn't pack anything I'd find "gross," even if, in her words, "Kelly, you need to open your mind to the joys of flavored cheese curls."

At the Monroe stop, we edge our way through crowds of business-casual people on their way home from work, Cubs fans on the way to Wrigley Field and buskers with acoustic guitars. We continue walking north down the platform until we're totally out of the space where the train stops. We could keep walking north all the way to Lake, but instead, we stop at the closed-down, abandoned Washington-Madison stop in between.

The word WASHINGTON is still engraved into the wall, though there aren't any other signs indicating which stop we're at. Non-functional elevators sit chained shut, and former exit doors are dark and blocked off. Though the cement floor is cracked and brown, it still seems cleaner than the other train stop floors since those are still walked on every day. To our left and right are the train tracks, except with no giant red sign with a train stop name. They still have those, "High Voltage! Keep off the tracks!" signs interspersed throughout. I guess they put them there because they know people like us walk in between the train stops sometimes, just to explore.

But I wonder if anyone else goes here for dates. Maybe we're the only couple weird enough for that. Though, Rebecca and Quentin going on a date here wouldn't surprise me.

Amber sets the grey backpack down on the floor and unzips her red hoodie. She takes it off in one swift motion, revealing the black Green Day T-shirt underneath.

"What year did you get that?" I ask her with a laugh.

She rolls her eyes at me but laughs softly. "It was one of the few clean shirts I had today. Judie calls these T-shirts 'leftovers from my 2000s emo phase.'"

"An accurate description."

Amber then lays her red hoodie out across the gross floor, and gestures for me to sit down.

"You want me to sit on your hoodie?"

"It's the closest thing I have to a picnic blanket or tablecloth or whatever."

I take a seat on her jacket. "Where are you going to sit."

She slides down onto the floor and sits cross-legged, facing me. "Oh, I couldn't give less of a fuck about how dirty this floor is. But, it struck me as something you'd care about."

So she's willing to put her jacket on an abandoned train station floor. I don't know if I'd ever want to say it out loud—for fear that she'll argue with me—but Amber really can be such a gentlelady sometimes.

Instead, I smile at her, and she smiles back.

"How do you manage to still fit into clothes you bought in middle school?" I ask, gesturing to her T-shirt.

"Two ways," she replies, pulling the backpack into her lap. "First, back in middle school, I bought tons of baggy clothes. Second, I haven't grown much since I was twelve anyway."

Then she unzips the backpack and pulls out our fancy date-night meal: a bag of tortilla chips, a bottle of barbecue sauce, and a bag of shredded Colby Jack cheese.

"We're having barbecue nachos!" she announces. "Since

they're one of my only weird foods that you don't hate. So I thought they could be, like, our *thing*."

She pulls out a Tupperware container, pulls open the bag of tortilla chips, and dumps the chips into the container. Then she rips open the bag of cheese and starts sprinkling it on top. "Don't worry," she says, not looking up from the cheese decorations she's making on the chips. "I stored this cheese in the mini-fridge under Samantha's desk today. It's not like I let it sit in my backpack all day or anything." Then she opens the barbecue sauce and starts drizzling zig-zags, loops, and other pretty patterns on top of the chips.

I guess, in a way, nachos are Amber's own personal form of art.

"That's pretty."

Amber laughs. "What? They're just nachos."

"There's no such thing as *just* nachos."

"I knew I liked you for a reason, Kelly from Marketing."

"No, I mean...like, nachos are to you what art is to me."

"So you're saying I'm a super talented nacho chef and should devote my life to making nachos?"

I shrug. "I don't devote my life to art. I wish I did, but I don't."

"Right. Because you work in marketing."

"I mean...marketing is its own kind of art. Its own way of bringing emotions to life through visual media."

She nods. "Yeah, I guess so." Then she stays quiet for a moment, just looking off into the empty distance. "Did I ever tell you I used to hate marketing?"

I have to hold myself back from bursting out laughing. "Not in those words, no. But I had a feeling."

"I don't hate it anymore. I mean, I *do* still hate a lot of things about it. Like, I hate how it emotionally manipulates a lot of people. Especially women. But I don't hate *you*. In fact, I the-opposite-of hate you. So...I guess what I'm trying to say is, you opened my mind. You showed me that something I hate doesn't have to be all bad."

I nod and shove a tortilla chip in my mouth. I don't really know what to say because I know I haven't been totally honest with Amber about everything. And I just hope she never thinks I'm emotionally manipulative, like the field I work in. I mean, I've never outright *lied* to her, either. But...I guess a lot of times, it's just clear to me that she has me on some kind of pedestal. I'm worried that the vision she has of me is better than who I actually am. If that even makes sense.

I don't know how to vocalize any of this, of course. Because despite how many times Amber compliments my confidence or tells me how smooth or irresistible I am, the truth is, I still feel painfully awkward inside. I still can't quite put my emotions into words.

So instead, I say, "Hey, by the way, next month I have a big art show at the Merchandise Mart. You should come."

27

AMBER

Ever since our weird, tragedy-stricken double date, Kelly seems different. At first, I'm not sure what it is.

The week after it happened, I just thought maybe she felt embarrassed about throwing up in front of me or something. But then we had our date at the abandoned train stop, and—don't get me wrong, it was romantic as hell—something about her seemed emotionally distant there. Like she couldn't tell me what was really going on in her head. Lots of awkward pauses.

But another week's nearly passed since then, and she's starting to look *physically* different, too. Not *super* different, mind you. It's almost like that time we showered together, and I freaked out because I saw how different she looked without makeup. She's still had makeup on, but she's just starting to change.

On Saturday, Judie and I hang out and watch sitcoms together, but even *that* feels different, too.

Like, I'm just smoking a bowl on the couch like I would on any normal Saturday, but Judie keeps saying things like,

"Ew, that smells gross," and, "Amber, smoking is so bad for you," and, "I don't want to get high from breathing your air."

"You can't get high from breathing my air, Judie. That's not how physics works." I'm a little surprised since I feel like Judie's been saying a lot fewer stupid things lately.

"What do *you* know about how physics works?"

I open my mouth, ready to say *Because I'm a woman in STEM*, or something, but then I realize it's way too easy for Judie to come up with a comeback for that. She'd just say something about how all I do is teach old people how to copy and paste, or remind them to re-start their computers, or tell them that it's "drag and drop," not "dragon drop." She'd tell me that even *she* could do my job, and I wouldn't have anything to say to that because she probably could.

Judie seems a little sad lately, too. I think it's because the Miz Lollipop tour was canceled. I'm pretty sure Betty J's still going on tour, but nobody really cares about just Betty J. Betty J's like a knockoff Miz Lollipop, or at least that's what Judie says.

I think she and Luke got a refund on the tickets, and are using the money to go on an expensive date at Venice Blues for Judie's birthday in February.

For the first time, I feel confident that one of Judie's relationships is going to last until February.

Are Kelly and I going to last until February?

I mean, logically, we should. There's nothing *wrong* with our relationship. Maybe we're just getting past the "honeymoon stage." Maybe we're just reaching the step where we watch Netflix on the couch together and yell about inside jokes when we're alone. Maybe the whole whirlwind romance part is done. Honestly, that's okay with me. Until Kelly, I'd never even thought romance was a real thing. I just thought it was something Judie made up to be dramatic or something marketing companies made up to sell expensive jewelry.

I guess in a sense, Kelly made me trust marketing more.

At our abandoned-train-stop date, I told her how she'd opened my mind. And I meant it; Kelly made me a better person. She helped me to grow and to see things beyond my own worldview. Maybe I said it casually, but it was *really* hard for me to say something like that out loud. I felt like I was opening myself up to her, becoming vulnerable.

And she didn't even respond to it.

Of course I'm going to go to her art show. I'm excited as hell for it. Kelly's art makes me *feel shit*. I guess Kelly's art is its own form of emotional manipulation. But, it's an emotional manipulation that feels good. Maybe Kelly's art is, like, what Judie would call *drugs*.

Over the course of our week at work, Kelly and I never make out in the bathroom. We do occasionally leave each other notes, but nothing too fancy. Just a few "Hey girl"s, maybe a few hearts drawn on a Post-it.

Still, I figure it's okay, right? Because, realistically, it's not like we could make out in the bathroom for the rest of our lives. Once we reached age forty or so, it wouldn't be cute anymore. Unless both of us aged as gracefully as Vivian Costello. Which, to be honest, Kelly probably will.

But I guess I thought we'd taper off gradually. Maybe

we'd start making out in the bathroom just twice a week, then once a week, then once or twice a month, *then* not at all.

It's not even like one of us is rejecting the other. We both just don't go to the bathroom as much anymore. Neither of us really takes the initiative to text the other about meeting up there. And when we are in there together, neither of us really makes the first move.

I've never had a relationship real enough to understand what's happening right now. I have nothing to compare this to. What is happening right now?

To an extent, it feels like Kelly's distancing herself from me. And I don't want to be the one to take too much initiative because I don't want to look desperate.

Leave it to Kelly to finally make me care what other people think of me.

Leave it to Kelly to turn my *whole fucking world* upside down and then half-disappear from my life.

Over the next few weeks, we still have dates. We watch sitcoms on my couch, sometimes with Judie and Luke. Sometimes we go to Crunchy's or take a walk around Downtown Chicago after work. Nothing super creative, though.

Kelly's been letting the blue streaks fade out of her hair. Maybe that's what's so different about her. I'm not sure I want to ask her about it because she hasn't brought anything up about it, and that sort of makes me think she doesn't want me to know.

Leave it to Kelly to make me start second-guessing every

stupid human interaction. Just like she did when she told me she liked my freckles.

Leave it to Kelly to make me see the world in ways no one else can.

Fuck. I really love Kelly.

During one date, as I stare across the Crunchy's table at Kelly, I notice that her face looks different. Not *that* different; her eyes are the same color, mouth is the same shape, all of that. But her cheeks have filled in *just a little*, like she's gained a little weight or something. But I don't know how Kelly could possibly gain weight, when she eats like a yoga mom.

Kelly never wants to have sex anymore, either. I stopped initiating after the second time she softly rejected me with no real reason given. I think maybe she's feeling insecure about her body or something. Maybe she *is* gaining some weight because every time I've seen her this past week, she's been wearing baggy hoodies like I wear.

She's gotta know I'd still find her sexy as hell, even if she gained weight. She *has* to know that I see her as so much more than how she looks. How, after all this time, can she not know that?

On Thursday night, three weeks and one day after our closed-down-train-stop date (not that I'm counting), I'm lying in my bed pondering all this. I'm stone-cold sober, balancing my laptop on my stomach, and staring at the ceiling. I don't even acknowledge the laptop; I was originally planning to watch lesbian accountant porn, but now I just can't get in any kind of sexual mood. The thought of sex makes me sad.

Then my laptop dings, and I see that I have an email notification from *The Feminist Forum*.

My article's been published.

28

AMBER

By Friday morning, my article's had 5,000 views.

For me, at least, that's a lot. I mean, Alice Gilbert's has over 40,000 right now, but none of mine have ever gotten more than a couple hundred. And that's even *with* me publicizing them on my Facebook *and* on Judie's Twitter and Instagram.

I guess people like this one.

Well, some do, some don't. I guess that's true of every article with a comment section.

"Tell your sister to stand the fuck up for herself," one commenter says.

To that, someone responds, "Okay, wow, *clearly* you've never had to deal with *legit* harassment. You can't always just stand up to men! They can get violent!"

And then those two argue for the next 20 comments about what it means to be an "empowered" woman, and if "empowered" women are expected to always stand up for themselves, and whether or not it was sexist to assume men were dangerous.

As I scroll down, the comment threads become less and less coherent, as they often do on the internet.

"ur sister is feeding in2 the patriarchyyyyy," says SciFiGirl94.

"Stop blaming society 4 ur own insicuraties," says DogLuvr3423, who does not know how to spell "insecurities."

So that's how I spend my morning in the basement of Costello's: reading comment wars on my article. Part of me takes a bit of a sick joy in reading the comments. I like how people are fighting over things I said. Not that I'm a fan of people fighting, or anything. But I am a fan of getting people to think, even if those thoughts lead to arguments.

Plus, comment-section drama never ceases to be entertaining.

I have to go up to the main floor once today. One of the guys who works on payroll forgets how to send a link. He's been sending a shortcut to where he had a file saved on his computer, not a link to the actual internet, and yells at me because he can't get the "link" to work.

So I click around on his computer a bit, copy-and-paste an actual link from an actual internet browser (Internet Explorer, in case that wasn't obvious), and he sends the email. It works. He's shocked, and tells me I must be magic. Yep, that's me.

On my way back to the staircase, I hear a familiar, demanding-yet-beautiful voice calling at me. "Amber! Can you help me for a second?"

I whip around to see Vivian Costello motioning for me to come towards her.

My heart rate picks up a little. I did not think Vivian Costello knew my name. I always thought she'd be one of those distant, removed bosses who'd call me "Amy" or "Anna" or a million other "A" names instead of Amber. But she knows me.

I don't know why I'm so nervous. It's not like I've even *thought* about my weird crush on Vivian Costello since I started dating the Eighth World Wonder that is Kelly.

Maybe it's that she's still my boss. Or that she's still got this super intimidating tone of voice that says, "*Don't you dare mess this up.*"

"Sure," I mumble, and walk towards her.

She hands me a small pile of documents. "Can you make fifty copies of each of these for me really quick? I'd do it myself, but I have a conference call. Drop them on my desk when you're done."

I should just say yes, make the copies, and go back downstairs, where I can continue reading comment wars and forget this ever happened. But instead, like the impulsive, no-filter blabbermouth that I am, I blurt out, "Isn't that Isabelle's job?"

But she's already walking away from me, just a blur of a form-fitting skirt suit, and bulging calves bolstered by velvet heels.

So I make the copies, drop them on her desk, and then rush back downstairs before Vivian Costello has another chance to run into me.

"DID ANYONE finish *Brian's Song* this week?" Rebecca asks at the book club meeting during lunch.

We all look at each other nervously. We've forgotten to start it.

"Oh, come on! It's been *three weeks*, guys! How did you forget to read a book *this short* three weeks in a row?!" Exasperated, Rebecca throws her arms up in the air.

"I watched the movie," Midge offers.

"Everyone's already seen the movie!" Rebecca counters.

"We have?" Kelly asks.

"All of us who *aren't* New York trash should've already seen it."

I watched it as a kid with my parents and Judie. It was a long, *long* time ago. After we watched it, I'd told my dad I wanted to play football when I grew up. He just ruffled my hair and told me girls can't play football. I think that was the first time I can remember feeling *anger*. Judie said she wanted to cheerlead, and then I remembered Mom saying something that implied Judie would have to get skinnier first. She didn't say it in those words exactly, but looking back, she was definitely implying it.

I'd forgotten about that memory until just now.

"So, I guess we weren't into that one," Rebecca sighs. "That's fine. Who's picking our next book again?"

"Isabelle is," says Tanya. "She promised us young-adult romance, and I'm so excited!"

"Yeah, but where *is* Isabelle?" asks Midge.

We all look around the room at each other, and realize that Isabelle isn't there. I guess she's sick or something. That's probably why Vivian Costello had me do her job. I'll have to figure out a way to tell Vivian Costello that I am not an intern. Maybe she knows that already. Maybe I should not attempt to get sassy with Vivian Costello. I don't know.

"Okay, well, without Isabelle here, I guess we still don't have a book to read then," says Rebecca, sliding down in her chair a little. She's looking more and more defeated by the second. It's making me sad; Rebecca always struck me as someone with an unbreakable spirit.

"I know," says Tanya. "How about for today, we read and discuss Amber's article?"

"What?!" I snap my head toward Tanya. "You subscribe to *The Feminist Forum*?"

Tanya shrugs. "Yeah, of course. What, did I not fit your image of what a feminist looks like?"

I stare at Tanya for a second. She's got thick, black curly hair and long eyelashes. She wears a bright fuchsia lipstick that pops against her dark complexion. She's dressed how she always is: business casual, but with a hyper-feminine flair. Today, it's a form-fitting grey tweed dress and shiny purple heels that almost match her lipstick. There's no denying it, Tanya's conventionally attractive. Of course, there's nothing about her that explicitly *doesn't* look like a feminist. I guess she just doesn't scream it like some of us (me) do.

"No, no, you do," I tell her. "What did you want to say about my article?"

"I didn't like it." She just lays it out there, direct and to-the-point. "I think you tried really hard to make it appeal to everyone. To be honest, you did a decent job addressing people who disagree with you, but that doesn't mean I've changed my mind. I think it's weird that you almost imply it's your sister's fault that men objectify her."

"That's not what I meant at all!" The time in our living room last month, when Judie told me I was victim-blaming her...that was the worst I'd ever felt in my life. "In my article, I explicitly said it was the *men's* fault!"

"But," Tanya continues, "right after you said that you didn't like how men are treating her like a prize, you went directly into saying that you don't support our cultural acceptance of Lipamorph. The juxtaposition of those lines implies that you think Lipamorph is part of the problem, and not gross men who need to keep their dicks out of your sister's business."

"I agree with Amber," says Fanny. "I don't think women over-sexualizing themselves is doing any good."

"Woah! Hold up, Fanny Spitzer!" I nearly yell. "That is not what I was saying. Did you even *read* my article?"

It feels a little uncomfortable to be getting aggressive in book club. But here we are.

"No, honey, I didn't read it," says Fanny. "I don't subscribe to your feminism website."

Of course she doesn't.

Basically ignoring Fanny, Tanya continues talking. "Also, the way you criticize its marketing. Like it's entirely the advertising industry's fault that women are making these choices. Aren't you *dating* a girl who works in marketing?"

I glance over at Kelly. Kelly is silent again. God, I hate this.

The rest of book club is just me and Tanya arguing. It's not nearly as fun as reading the comment section on my article.

Before we know it, our lunch break is up, and everyone's getting up to leave. Samantha immediately turns back to her computer. Midge, Tanya, Rebecca, and Fanny make their way out the door. Kelly stays for a moment.

"Amber," she says quietly. "Not here, not now, but...but we need to talk."

29

JUDIE

Luke can tell I've been down ever since Miz Lollipop's overdose. Like I said, Luke can always tell when I'm sad, and he always knows how to make me feel better. He's a good guy.

We've been going out a lot these past few weeks. On Friday evenings, we've started going bar-hopping in Wicker Park along with Michelle and Mikayla. Michelle and Mikayla like Luke, too. I think they're actually a little jealous of me since they haven't found guys as nice as Luke yet. I'll admit, I'm pretty lucky.

I've met a few of Luke's friends, too. Tom and Bill and Peter, the guys he went to college with, sometimes come out with us to the bars. Luke's glad we can all hang out in a big group since he hasn't had as much time to see Tom, Bill, and Peter ever since taking ownership of Big Mama's.

Then, on Sunday afternoons, Luke and I just watch TV on the couch, either at his place, or at my and Amber's place. But I like going to his place better because he has a cappuccino machine, and we can experiment with different coffee flavors.

Today's Sunday, and I've been super excited to go to Luke's all day. Partially for the cappuccinos, and partially—I'm sort of sad to admit this—because I kind of want to get away from Amber.

Don't get me wrong, I love my sister, but these past few days she's just been such a *downer*. Apparently this past Friday, Kelly said the Four Words of Doom to her: "We need to talk."

They still haven't talked, but I think they're planning to go out later tonight and finally do it. I don't know what's taking them so long, but I can tell Amber's nervous. I don't blame her. I like Kelly, too. She's good for Amber. Amber's been a lot less annoying since they got together.

Luke and I make salted caramel mocha cappuccinos together in small white ceramic mugs. The kind with the tiny handles that you can only fit one or two fingers through. Then we take them over to the black couch in his living room and sit down. I reach for the remote to turn the TV on, but he grabs my hand and stops me.

"Judie," he says, "is everything...okay?"

I take a sip of my cappuccino, letting the mix of sweet, savory, and bitter flavors warm my tongue. "What do you mean?"

He sighs. "I mean...look, I know you've been really sad since the whole thing with Miz Lollipop. And I get it. Believe it or not, I might've been almost as excited for that concert as you were."

I have to laugh at that. "For real? I guess I really converted you, then."

"I won't lie. You *really* turned me on to 'Worship Dat Booty.' That song is catchy as hell. I don't even mind when it gets stuck in my head anymore."

I keep smiling. "I'm glad. I've never been able to get Amber to appreciate the joys of Miz Lollipop, so I'm happy you do."

Luke nods, but then his smile disappears. "Judie...I know you're sad about her. But I get this feeling that that's not *all* it is."

I swallow another sweet-but-salty sip of my drink. "What do you mean?"

He slides his arm around my shoulders and makes perfect eye contact with me. "I mean...Miz Lollipop's great, but she's a famous person you don't even know. I can't help but think that your sadness is more about *you*. Are you worried? About overdosing or anything?"

I sit there, just drinking my coffee and thinking for a second. Luke's ultra-perceptiveness strikes again. Overdosing has been a worry in the back of my mind. But since Miz Lollipop is the only big overdose story, and she's been taking insane amounts of it for years, I don't know how much I have to worry about. But now I know that it's a possibility, the fear is definitely there.

"Yeah, I guess I am a little," I answer, fiddling with the tiny handle on my mug. I stare down into the light-brown, foamy liquid. "But not, like, *that* worried. I only take it a few times a week at most. Usually just once a week. Only an extra time if I want to give myself an extra edge, for like a special occasion or something."

"I'm gonna level with you, Stiles," says Luke. His arm is still draped over my shoulders, and his hand pats my shoulder a little. "I'm worried for you. But, like you said, not *super* worried. I do trust that you're smart enough to know when enough's enough. And I don't want to tell you how you can and can't look. That would never be fair of me. I love the way you look. I just don't want you to ever risk your health for it. Just promise me you'll be safe about it."

I smile at him. "I promise I will."

Then, as I take the next sip of my coffee, I smile to myself. Because Luke's the first person to ever say that phrase to me. "I trust that you're smart enough."

30

AMBER

Sunday night at Crunchy's with Kelly, I'm eating The Amber, like usual. It's no secret that it's kind of a messy burger to eat, but today I'm struggling more than usual. My hands have been shaking a little, and some of the Fritos have fallen out onto my plate. A few times, I've accidentally squeezed a few drips of barbecue sauce out from in between the buns, and it's creating a big mess.

Kelly's eating a salad.

So far, it's all been meaningless small talk. How we've been this weekend. What we've been up to today. How work's going. All the stuff we presumably already know about each other, but still waste our time talking about so that we don't have to address the difficult stuff.

I swallow a big lump of burger, and take the plunge. "What was it you wanted to talk about?"

Kelly stares down at her salad. Her bangs fall in front of her glasses a little, and I notice that all the blue streaks have totally faded. She still looks beautiful, like always. And, again like always, how she looks is not my top concern. Even though I am a little concerned by how her face has filled out just a little, and how she's wearing one of Rebecca's oversized Cubs jerseys.

Come to think of it, I haven't seen Kelly dress business-casual in weeks.

She pauses for a moment before answering. I see her pick at her salad a little. She stabs a cherry tomato with her fork, and I watch as a thin stream of red juice drizzles out.

"You're going to judge me," she says, her voice even. "I've been trying to avoid a fight with you because you've always struck me as someone I don't want to fight with. But it's too late now."

Everything comes together right then.

Honestly, I don't know how I was so stupid I didn't notice it before. As the past two months flash by in my mind, the signs were there. One after the other, staring me in the face. And I refused to acknowledge them. Because, in my mind...I couldn't allow myself to see Kelly as anything less than perfect. My idea of perfect.

I take a deep breath in through my nose. "You've been using Lipamorph, haven't you?"

Not looking up from her salad, she nods.

It's starting to make sense. How her body started changing right after she learned of Miz Lollipop's overdose. How she started hiding her body from me in the interest of avoiding a fight. How she never once took my side during any of our book club arguments.

But one thing's still throwing me.

"But...I only saw your body change back. I never saw it change in the first place."

She looks up at me then. "What do you mean?"

"I mean...you're clearly not taking it anymore now, right? I'm assuming because now you know of the overdose possibilities?"

She nods. "Yeah. When I saw what happened to Miz Lollipop, I decided it wasn't worth the risk."

"Right. So, when did you *start* taking it? I never noticed your body change in the first place."

"I started taking it before I met you. You never saw my body without it until now."

I think back to that day we met in the bathroom and how that was only two days after the very first Lipamorph commercial aired. The one with the giant SCULPT YOURSELF letters, and the creepy blonde model, and the intense lighting.

"But it was barely even out before I met you."

She continues staring at me. Her mouth twitches a little, like she wants to talk, but she's worried about what to say.

"Amber..." she starts. Her nervousness is immediately apparent in the way her eyes dart down towards her salad. "I got it early. Me and a few of the other girls in my office. We got it a few months ago."

"How?"

"Because." Then she swallows, like what she's about to tell me is an even bigger deal than what she already admitted to me.

If that's even possible.

"Because Finnegan & Peters ran its marketing campaign."

My stomach tightens. I look down at my burger and suddenly understand how someone could think it looks gross. The crushed-up Fritos and splatters of barbecue sauce lay on my plate like a murder scene.

"It was *you* all along? It was *you* doing all that manipulative marketing? It was *you* making women feel like they had to chemically alter their bodies to be desirable?"

"No!" she shouts, slamming the table. It startles me a little. A few other Crunchy's patrons glance at us. "It wasn't me. It wasn't even my team. The Lipamorph project was almost entirely handled by the Visual Marketing department in our *Los Angeles* office. The Chicago office barely did anything but listen in on a few conference calls. I wasn't even assigned to that project. The whole time it was underway, Rebecca and I were busy working on a billboard campaign for Venice Blues. I had nothing to do with *any* of those commercials. Our company just all got early access to Lipamorph as a perk."

I nod, unsure of what to say. Kelly didn't make those commercials, sure. But she watched them happen. I'm conflicted. Because of course Kelly couldn't have done anything to stop them. It wasn't her place. And Kelly clearly loves her job.

Samantha's words echo in my head again. *This isn't as black and white as we want it to be.*

"Why didn't you tell me?"

Kelly gives me one of those sarcastic half-laughs. "Forgive me, but after all those times you talked about it at our book club, and then after that article you wrote...it just didn't seem like you'd be cool with it."

"Well, if I'm being totally honest," (which is a lot more than Kelly ever did for me), "I'm *not* all that cool with it. It does kind of bother me that my amazing girlfriend thinks she needs to chemically alter her body in order to look good."

"Oh, shut up!" she practically shouts, punctuating her statement with the slam of her fork against her salad plate. "Who are you to judge me for chemically altering my body? You think I don't know you were high on our first date?"

"What?" She's right—I didn't think she knew that.

"I could smell it in your hair, you dummy. And *sure*, at first I was a little insulted because it felt like getting high was more important to you than our date. But then I realized, you were probably just nervous. And if that's what you needed to do to feel better, who am I to stop you? That's all I did. I did what I needed to feel better about my body."

"I'm a little insulted, too, if I'm being totally honest," I say since we're no longer holding anything back. "Insulted that you weren't comfortable with me seeing you how you naturally look."

"*Naturally?*" Another one of those insincere laughs. "Are you kidding me right now? Do you remember the first thing you said to me? It was either, 'I like your hair,' or 'I like your nails.' This may come as a shock to you, Amber, but blue hair and green nails aren't *natural* either."

I'm not sure what to say to that because she's totally right. Kelly's always right. Kelly could argue circles around me; I'm not sure why she was so afraid of *me* during a fight. So I just let her continue talking.

"And don't forget," she says, "you were the one who was attracted to me. Altered body and all. You *liked* my body. You *made love* to my body, when it was *altered*."

Like five more people stare at us. We're *that* couple right now. Arguing in front of a million people and making a big scene.

"But you lied to me, Kelly."

She shakes her head. "I didn't. I just presented myself to you the way I'm happiest. It wasn't any more of a lie than my blue hair was."

I have so many things I want to ask her. I want to ask her why she altered her body to traditionally patriarchal standards. But it doesn't matter because I was the one who was attracted to her, and I'm a woman. I want to ask her if these past few weeks, she's refused sex because she's insecure about her natural body or because she was trying to keep me from finding out, so that she could avoid fighting with me.

But my brain's fried. So I just ask, "What are you going to do now?"

"What do you mean?"

"Are you keeping your body like this, or what?"

"Does it matter to you?"

I don't know how to answer that. I just stare at Kelly who, until today, I've never seen look this vulnerable before.

After a long moment of silence passes, she looks up at me. "I'm not what you expected, right?"

"I still love you, Kelly," I sigh. "But you kept so many

things from me. So technically, yeah, you're not what I expected."

"You expected someone much more confident. Someone much more sure of herself. Someone smart, and pretty, and perfect. I give off that vibe for some reason. I don't know why. Zack was confused about me, too, and that was before Lipamorph was even a thing. Everyone always expects that I'm so much more than I am. And then in the end, I'm always a big disappointment."

I stare at Kelly's sad eyes—the same green, gold-flecked eyes that used to stare at me seductively from inside bathroom stalls.

What should I say? I can't lie and say I'm not disappointed. But at the same time, she's right. I *did* idealize her into so much more than she was. More than any person could be, really. Maybe that's just what falling in love for the first time feels like.

I guess I stay silent for too long because after a few minutes, Kelly takes a big nervous breath. "Let's take a break, Amber."

Then she throws a ten-dollar bill onto the table, to pay for the salad, and leaves.

Because she's too nervous to handle the fallout. She just turns away from me and runs out because she's afraid of how I'll react.

She's right; I had all kinds of wrong ideas about her.

31

AMBER

Monday in the basement of Costello's, I'm chugging lemon-lime Gatorade like I'm trying to fight the world's biggest hangover. Despite the fact that I drank zero alcohol and smoked zero weed last night.

I guess break-ups can give you a hangover, too.

I want to reflect on this. To question why Kelly felt the need to end things. To brainstorm ideas of how to convince her we should get back together. To ask myself what changes I need to make in order to be someone she *wants* to get back together with.

But right now, all I can do is stare at the ceiling and drink Gatorade.

Then another worry hits me: what am I going to do when I need to pee out all this Gatorade? I don't want to use this bathroom since I have a major chance of running into Kelly in there. But Kelly's probably thinking the same thing, so she's probably just going to use the bathroom on her own floor. I hope.

Then, something that almost never happens on a Monday morning happens. My ugly landline phone rings.

"Hello, this is Amber from Tech Support, how can I help you?"

"Hey, Amber! It's Vivian."

I never thought of Vivian Costello as just a "Vivian." She never seemed like a first-name basis type of person. I also never pictured her saying, "Hey, Amber!" or even "hey." But I guess the theme of these past few days has been realizing that my preconceived notions about pretty much everything are wrong, so at least it's fitting.

"Oh, hi. What can I do for you?" Do I call her Vivian? Do I say Ms. Costello? Why is that nervous feeling taking over my body again?

"Can you just come up here? I need help with a few things."

"Okay. Sure. Be right there."

I rush up the stairs, silently praying that I won't run into Kelly in the stairwell. If she's using the bathroom on her own floor to avoid *me*, I shouldn't need to worry. But if there's anything the past few days have taught me, it's that I can't predict Kelly's behavior. That I don't know Kelly as well as I thought I did.

When I reach Vivian Costello's office, she hands me a giant stack of papers. "These need to be filed in that cabinet over there." She points to a filing cabinet across the room. "Clients' names will be sorted alphabetically. Each paper should have the name of the client on it. They're the fourth-quarter tax returns. I need to get them filed by the end of the day."

I stare at her for a second. "You...you know my job is tech support, right?"

"Yes, Amber," she sighs. "I know what I hired you for. But could you just do this for me? As a favor?"

I nod. "Yeah, sure. Of course. But, I just mean...where's Isabelle?"

"She's in the hospital for a few days," she says. "They're not sure when she's going to be out yet. We can't get behind here. So I figured, you're paid hourly, and Isabelle wasn't paid at all, so you might as well just do it while you're here."

"Yeah, yeah...I mean, that's fine, no problem." I'm just nodding like a stupid bobblehead. "I just mean...I hope she's okay."

Vivian nods. "I do too. The call I had with her mom this morning sounded kind of serious. Some kind of medication overdose."

I don't know what to say to that, so I just stupidly nod again, and then take the stack of papers from Vivian.

I SPEND the rest of the day filing papers for Vivian, and occasionally stepping away when some old guy taps me on the shoulder and tells me his internet broke again. Then I go home.

It's weird, not seeing Kelly after work, or in the bathroom, or anywhere at all. It's weird just staring out the window on the Purple Line ride home. It's weird having no one to text when I see a vegetarian food truck that looks kind of good. We only dated about two months, but life without Kelly is already weird.

That's when I realize that it's almost November, meaning Kelly's art show is coming up. Do I still go to it? Part of me says definitely not since seeing Kelly is going to feel like getting punched in the gut. But the other part of me really wants to see her art. Because her art is beautiful, and it's what helped me learn to appreciate things for their aesthetic. My Purple Line train car passes the Merchandise Mart, and I think about seeing Kelly's art in there. Giant portraits of her cat on display. Or maybe more of those coffee-stain napkin doodles she showed me.

As the train leaves the Downtown area and heads back toward the North Side, I just keep staring out the window and thinking, and I eventually get to thinking about Isabelle. At first, it's kind of selfish thinking because I'm a little worried that Vivian Costello is going to make me do all of Isabelle's work until she gets back. Which I guess is okay because Isabelle does more work than I do and doesn't get paid. But Isabelle's job is also boring as hell.

But then I start worrying about Isabelle herself—mainly, wondering what her overdose was like. Wondering if she had to get a limb amputated like Miz Lollipop did. Wondering if anyone in our book club knows what hospital she's in, so maybe we can go visit her or something. Then, wondering if she *wants* to be visited. What does she look like in there?

Isabelle's only crime was wanting to be taken seriously in the workplace. She just wanted respect. It's not her fault that everyone judged her on the fact that she looked like a twelve-year-old.

And I guess that's when I kind of realize that it's *no one's* fault. It's not Lipamorph's fault for giving her access to a drug that could fix that problem, especially because the drug was necessary for people like Samantha's cousin. It's not even Finnegan & Peters's fault for creating a marketing campaign that made it look so desirable because that's what marketing *does*. And I can hate it all I want, but it's still an industry that exists.

In pondering whose fault this whole thing is, I decide that it's probably kind of everyone's fault. Even mine.

32

KELLY

I CAN LIE TO MYSELF ALL I WANT, BUT IT'S POINTLESS. I miss Amber.

I miss her when I look at Sienna, and think about how she used to snuggle up in my green armchair with her. And then I think about Sienna's fur being burnt sienna, and how Amber's hair and eyes and freckles are all a dark shade of amber.

I'm not sure yet if I regret breaking up with her. It does feel good to no longer hide things from her. And it feels *great* to have all my feelings out in the open—how I felt she idealized me, how she couldn't see my flaws.

But it also feels bad to think about the breakup at all.

So once I get home from work on Monday, I immediately close myself up in my art studio with Sienna. I get a jazz playlist going on my laptop, and continue working on one of the pieces for my upcoming art show.

I sit at the desk Zack built me, with my pile of red adobe clay, and my sketchbook open to one of my anatomy studies pages. I prop my sketchbook up against the wall so I can stare at it while I work with the clay. I stare at my sketches: the three girls from outside of West Loop College, who turned themselves into surrealist sculptures. I'm doing a series of actual sculptures based on them, with accompanying drawings.

I want to call my piece "Sculpt Yourself." But it feels a little bit treasonous to call it that since I work for the company that came up with that slogan. And now I'm stealing it for the purpose of a half-satire.

I lose myself in the sculpture for a few hours, until I notice the sky getting darker outside the window, and Sienna starts clawing at my chair to tell me it's dinner time.

After I feed Sienna, I sit down in my green armchair with my sketchbook in my lap, and stare at the half-finished sculpture on the desk in front of me. It's the bobblehead girl, with a ton of fat in her face, but none almost anywhere else. I've sculpted her into a 12-inch figure, with a giant head, giant feet, and giant calves. The rest of her body is thin and narrow. I've even tried to capture the ribs jutting out of her abdomen, but that part could use some more work.

Then I flip through my sketchbook a little. I'm going to finish the sculptures of all three girls, but then I'm going to do some drawings and paintings to go along with them. One of the paintings I'm working on is sitting on the other side of my desk, leaned up against the wall. It's an oil painting on an 18x24 canvas of Jessica from page 14 of *Playboy*, but I'm setting her on the cover of a fictitious magazine (the title of which I have yet to decide), and I'm giving her some neon, pop-art style coloring. Like Warhol, I guess. Not to be too cliché or anything.

As I'm flipping through the pages, trying to figure out what other drawings I can pair with these, I find my sketch of Amber. I don't want to think about her right now, so I flip way back to the front.

And, of course, there I find my sketch of Zack. I drew him two years ago, right after I got this sketchbook. That was senior year of college, just eight months before we broke up because I was moving to Chicago.

Zack and I dated for three years. *Three years.* That's a long time. If we weren't still in college, we probably would've gotten married or something.

Probably. I'm not sure. Zack and I had the same problem that Amber and I did: he refused to see me beyond his perfected ideal.

Maybe I'm the problem.

I pick my cell phone up off the desk and impulsively call Zack. I haven't talked to him in months, even though we promised to stay friends when I moved away. We actually did do a good job of staying friends after we broke up, the last couple months before I moved here.

The phone rings in my ear, and I start second-guessing myself. Maybe I shouldn't call Zack. What am I even gonna say to him? *Why* am I calling him? Because I miss Amber and I'm lonely? Because I saw a picture of him in my sketchbook?

"Kelly?"

"Hey, Zack."

"Hey, how are you doing? It's been a while!"

I can hear the smile in his voice. Zack always had that kind of voice. You could tell when he was smiling. Which was frequently.

"I'm okay," I tell him. Then, it just all comes out. I tell him *everything*: my relationship with Amber, how I lied to her by omission about so many things, how everybody's fighting over a drug that my company publicized, my breakup with Amber, and finally, my upcoming art show. Then, I finish it all off with the million-dollar question. "Why does everybody think I'm so much cooler than I am?"

Zack bursts out laughing at that. "Okay, Kelly. Calm down and let me process *all* of that, okay?"

That's when I realize that I just ranted to him for twenty minutes straight. "Sorry," I mumble.

"No, no, it's cool! I'm actually honored that you see me as the kind of ex you can talk to about your current relationships."

I let out a slow, even exhale. I'm surprised how easily Zack and I can still talk after all this time. "I hope I'm that kind of ex for you, too."

"Oh, definitely," he agrees. "You were never the jealous type. At least that I saw. Maybe you were, and I just thought you were cooler than you actually are, like you said." He laughs a little again. "But yeah, I can tell you all about Heather, the new girl I've been seeing, if you want. But I'd rather focus on that big brain dump you just took."

"Actually, tell me about Heather."

And he does. He tells me all about Heather, who's about

to start medical school. She wants to be a brain surgeon. They've been dating for about three months now, and she's introduced him to golf.

"You know," he says, "Heather's always saying things like, 'Oh, I must be boring you so much with my MCAT studying' and stuff, but she never does bore me. Maybe some people are just like that. Like you and Heather, I mean."

"Like what?"

"Like...you just said that I thought you were cooler than you actually were, right? And that Amber thought that too? I don't think that's how it is. I think maybe you just don't realize how cool you are."

"Maybe."

"No, listen. I'm like 90% sure of this. Kelly, you're working in marketing, making a butt-load of money, and spending almost all of your free time making art good enough to be featured in a big Downtown Chicago art show. Like, I don't care who you are, that's *objectively cool*."

"Thanks." I pause for a moment, processing everything Zack just said. "But I don't get why Amber had so many wrong ideas about me then. Like that I was this perfectly confident lady who wanted to fight for all of the same feminist causes she did. Or that I was—"

"Because you're not communicating well," Zack cuts me off. "You and I had that problem too, and I'll chalk it up to us being immature college kids. Maybe it's because Heather's dad is a therapist, but she's been *perfect* at communication in the relationship. You just have to be honest with Amber.

Tell her everything. Including whether or not you want to give the relationship another try."

"Maybe *you* should be a therapist," I laugh.

"If the whole accountant thing doesn't work out, I'll keep it in mind." I can still hear the smile in his voice.

33

AMBER

Before I met Kelly, Monday nights were for rum, Coke, shitty sitcoms, and occasionally a joint.

After I met Kelly, Monday nights were for running around Chicago and going on quirky, indie rom-com style adventures.

Now, I guess Monday nights are for drinking and TV again. I think my midlife crisis might come early.

I flop on my back on the living room couch and turn on *Everybody Loves Raymond*. One of the first things I see is Frank telling Marie to get back into the kitchen, so I instantly start guzzling the cup of rum and Coke I have on the end table next to me.

Judie's at Luke's tonight, so I'm all on my own for this.

I set my cup back down on the end table and slide my phone out of the back pocket of my skinny jeans.

"Frank just told Marie to get back in the kitchen," I text Brianne.

"Did you take a shot?" she replies.

"Well, it was a mixed drink. But in spirit." Then, I take another drink.

My phone lights up a few seconds later. "Want to watch together?" Brianne asks.

So I call her, and put her on speaker phone.

"Hold on, which episode are you on?" she asks, out loud this time. "I'll get it up on Netflix."

Hearing Brianne's voice again feels better than I expected. I picture her sitting on the couch of her small Iowa apartment, legs crossed with her feet tucked under her. She'd probably be under some kind of quilt as well. Probably the patchwork quilt her mom gave her our final year of college. She's probably got her thick black hair piled in a bun on top of her head, and her wire-framed glasses perched on her nose. She only wears the glasses when she's at home and sick of wearing contacts.

"Hey, I miss you," I blurt out, instantly regretting it. That definitely came out 80% more flirty than I intended. Well, I guess to be accurate, it came out infinity times more flirty than I intended it because I didn't intend it to be flirty at all.

"I miss you too," she says. "No one in Iowa wants to watch bad sitcoms. No one that I've met yet, anyway. They all just watch, like, *Game of Thrones* and shit."

"To be fair, there are probably plenty of drinking games you can make to go along with that show."

Brianne laughs. "You shrugged right then, didn't you? I could hear it in your voice."

Then I start laughing, too. "You're a five-hour drive away, and you still know me better than anyone else."

"You too, girl."

Then an awkward silence hits us. It seems to last hours, but it definitely doesn't last more than a minute or so because the whole time I can hear one of Raymond and Debra's fights in progress on the TV in the background.

"Hey, so, I know we don't really talk about dating or anything much, but...I'm a mess, Brianne."

"Because of me?"

"What? No. I mean, I miss you and everything. But I had a girlfriend. Kelly. We just broke up last night."

"Oh, God, Amber. I'm so sorry to hear that."

We've stopped paying attention to *Everybody Loves Raymond* and just started drinking consistently.

"Thanks. I'm just, like...not sure about anything anymore. Like, do we get back together? The majority of me wants to, but I don't think any of her wants to. And then the small part of me that doesn't want to keeps saying that she wasn't the girl I thought she was because she lied to me about so many things, but then the bigger part of me says, 'Do any of the things she lied about even really matter?'"

"Wow. This may be above my paygrade."

"It's only above your paygrade until you drink enough."

Brianne laughs at that, and I can hear her take another sip of whatever she's drinking out there in Iowa. Probably a vodka lemonade.

"Look, Amber," she says, clearly a little drunk. "You know I'm not the best person for relationship advice. I haven't even figured myself out yet."

"You haven't?" When I laugh at that, I realize that I've

gotten a little bit drunk too. "Brianne, come on. We banged like six times."

"I remember. But I also remember all the weed that was involved. And then I remember Jake..."

"You still talk to Jake?"

"Here and there."

"Okay. Well, no offense or anything, but if you're still trying to figure yourself out, I'm not sure Iowa is the place to do it."

"Girl, you've never even been to Iowa."

"And I plan to keep it that way. Get your ass to Chicago."

Then we laugh for a few moments, followed by another lengthy awkward silence.

"All I'm saying," she says, suddenly sounding like she's sobered up, "is that I'm probably the worst person to help you fix your relationship with Kelly. But if you want to stay with her, and she's willing to get drunk and watch stupid-ass sitcoms with you, then I say hold onto that girl for dear life."

"Thanks, Brianne."

"You smiled just then! I heard it in your voice."

34

JUDIE

In the days leading up to the first of November, Luke and I are frantically cleaning every inch of Big Mama's Coffee.

"Half the time, you forget when the health inspector's even supposed to come," I laugh. "But you go crazy just because your *mom's* coming."

"This is Paulina we're talking about, Stiles," Luke says, scrubbing the counter with a freshly laundered rag and some cleaning solution I've never heard of. "*The* Big Mama!"

I halfheartedly push some chairs into some tables as I walk around the cafe, watching Luke freak out over small coffee splatters on the counter, or crumbs near the trash cans.

"Judie, this is the first time she's visited the coffee shop *she* started since she moved back to Greece. And it's not only that, but it's also the first time I'm introducing my mom to my girlfriend. Do you see how the stress is reasonable?"

I didn't even think about it that way. About how I'm Luke's girlfriend, meeting his mom for the first time. I guess it didn't even cross my mind because there's no way in hell I'll ever introduce Luke to my mom. Back in high school, even Michelle and Mikayla were afraid of her.

"Do you think she'll like me?"

Luke lets out a big, hearty laugh at that. "There's no question. Hell, she'll probably like you more than she likes me. You two will probably become best friends and start ganging up on me. Trust me, it's not *you* who needs to worry."

"Then I won't." And with that, I stop cleaning, and head to the back room to go put on a new playlist. This morning, Miz Lollipop was released from the hospital, and I'm gonna celebrate.

On the morning of the first, I wake up a little earlier than usual. I want to have time to get dressed and make myself look awesome for Luke's mom.

As I'm squeezing into one of my form-fitting knit sweater dresses, I wonder if I should take a pill today. I've only taken one this week, so it probably can't hurt. At the same time, I've been more and more nervous to take them since I saw what happened to Miz Lollipop.

The week after Miz Lollipop went to the hospital, Amber kept telling me I'd be an idiot to keep taking Lipamorph. So I asked her, what about all those people who smoke too much weed and jump off a bridge? I think, in that moment, she understood the concept of *moderation*. And that I can hold my own in an argument against her.

Either that or she was just too upset by her breakup with Kelly to bother arguing with me anymore.

I'm sad that Amber and Kelly broke up, too. I wanted them to have more double dates with me and Luke.

Plus, also, in all my twenty-two years as Amber's sister, I've never seen her as happy as I've seen her with Kelly.

I decide to take the extra pill, just so I can move a little bit of the extra fat off of my stomach. I've been a little bloated this week, and I want to make sure everything looks proportional, the way I like it. I promise myself no more pills this week. Not that I'll need them. Nor have I been exceeding two pills a week since I heard about Miz Lollipop.

Then, I spend twenty minutes in front of the mirror crafting the perfect smoky eye and putting on some neon-pink lipstick. I hit my hair with the curling iron, just enough to make some pretty waves, and then head out to work. On the way out, I catch a glimpse of myself in the hallway mirror. Wavy hair, perfect face, light-grey sweater dress, dark purple leggings, and knee-high caramel-colored boots. If you didn't know any better, you'd think I worked at Venice Blues.

"You must be Judie the Cutie!"

That's the first thing I hear when I walk through the front door of Big Mama's. I look forward, and see a dark-haired middle-aged woman running toward me. She immediately wraps her arms around my waist, pulls me into a hug so powerful that she lifts my feet off the ground, and spins me in a circle.

"You must be..." Paulina? Luke's mom? Big Mama?

"You can call me Paulina!" she says. "Or Big Mama if you prefer. Ever since little Lukie grew up, no one's really called me that. But I do sometimes miss it!" Paulina puts me back down on the floor. "Oh, Judie. I've seen so many pictures of you on the Facebook. You're even more adorable in person!"

"Aw, thank you."

I stare at Paulina. That's when it hits me. Big Mama is *big*.

Not that it should be a surprise. I guess she wouldn't have gotten that nickname if she'd been a little stick like Amber. Or maybe she would've, if her family has an ironic sense of humor. But when I say she's big, I mean *big*. I mean, even if she took Lipamorph, which I doubt she does (it's only been released in the US, UK, and China so far, so they don't have it in Greece), she would still be big everywhere. She's got a big smiling face, a giant tummy like Luke's, and huge thighs, all of which is covered in a brown tweed pantsuit.

I guess I'd always sort of assumed that Big Mama wasn't big. I figured if she *were* a large lady, people wouldn't call her Big Mama. That would be mean, right? Isn't it rude to draw attention to how large someone is?

That's at least what I always thought. Every time in middle school when Amber punched someone for calling me fat, it was because they'd used "fat" as an insult. Every time in high school my mom wouldn't let me leave the house in a crop top, it was because my stomach was showing. And I was supposed to hide that.

Every time I'd stand in front of the school bathroom

mirror and say, "I feel fat today," Michelle and Mikayla would always tell me I wasn't fat at all. That I just wasn't one of those *skinny bitches*. But that made me feel kind of bad, too, because Amber was undoubtedly a skinny bitch, and I didn't like *her* being made fun of, either.

I guess this is the first time I've met a woman who *wants* to draw attention to her size. And I'm really, really curious about it. A big part of me wants to ask her why she's called Big Mama. Who came up with the name? Did she? Was it, like, a reclaimed slur from her childhood? Would Amber be shocked that I know what *reclaimed slur* means?

But something still feels awkward about asking her. Maybe I will later, after we get to know each other better.

Big Mama, or I guess I should call her Paulina, wanders around the coffee shop for a few minutes, inspecting everything. I don't know why Luke was so afraid of her; she doesn't seem like she has a critical bone in her body.

(Well, okay, I'm sure she has *critical* bones in her body, like a spine and a skull and whatnot, but I mean, I don't think she's capable of criticizing people. It's an expression! I think.)

I end up being wrong about that.

Once our morning rush of customers comes in, Paulina has all *kinds* of things to say to Luke.

"What, no 'have a nice day' before she walks out the door? What kind of customer service is that?"

"Lukie! You don't need to ask *Greta* if she wants room for cream! She's been coming here every day since the 90s!"

I guess it's fair. After all, she is *the* Big Mama. This is her coffee shop, her vision, her baby. She doesn't criticize me at all. In fact, there's really only one thing she says to me.

"Judie, you've got a lovely smile. No wonder you guys have so many regulars."

I like Paulina.

I like the way she struts around the cafe like she owns the place, even though she hasn't technically owned the place for a few years now. I like how she makes criticism sound like a compliment. (An art my own mom was never able to master.) I like how everything she says comes from a place of sincerity, and you can see it in her eyes and hear it in her voice.

I think I understand what Luke means: about how confidence is an attractive quality. I guess I feel kind of bad saying this, but for a while, I forget she's fat. Not that it's something I need to *remember*. Not that it's the most important thing about her. It's just that...her personality is so much bigger than she is.

Paulina heads out that evening. "Lukie, I will see you tonight when you get home. Remember to lock everything up. And clean all the cappuccino machines. And—"

"Mom, I've been running this place for years. You don't need to remind me."

She points one long, red-polished finger right at him. "That's Big Mama to you, Lukie. Judie, it was a pleasure to meet you. I'll see you tomorrow."

Paulina is staying on the couch at Luke's apartment for the week so that she can save money on hotel costs.

As soon as Paulina leaves, Luke gets to work cleaning

the cappuccino machine. I sit on the counter, my back to any potential customers, and face Luke.

He smiles at me. "I told you she'd like you."

I pause for a moment, thinking about what I'm going to ask. "Luke...your mom...the whole Big Mama thing..."

He stops cleaning the cappuccino machine and turns around to face me. "What do you mean?"

"I mean..." I try so hard to think of how to phrase what I want to say but nothing eloquent comes to mind, so all my thoughts just spill out like vomit. "Did she give herself that nickname? Or did someone else? And was she always fat or did she get fat when she got older? And was she always that confident or did that happen when she got older too? And was Big Mama like a self-deprecating humor type of thing, or was it more of a reclaimed slur? And..."

"Judie." Luke places his hands gently on my shoulders, and I suddenly remember to breathe. "Yes," he continues. "She's always been fat. Big Mama was the name she gave herself after she had me since she was big and a mom. It started off like a joke, you know. Like, she'd call herself 'The Big Mama,' because she was my mom, and she raised a lot of my cousins, too, while their parents were at work. Then when she opened the coffee shop, she let us hang out there, and she kept an eye on us, so she was kind of a mom and a coffee shop owner at the same time. So, Big Mama's Coffee. And as far as her being confident...yeah, as far back as I can remember, she always has been."

When I get home that night, I don't have a drink, I don't watch shitty sitcoms, and I don't argue with Amber about anything. Instead, I just lie in bed and think. I think about Paulina, and how before her, I'd never met anyone who *owned* being fat like she did. How I'd never met anyone who made a conventionally-imperfect body *seem* perfect through her confidence. And then I think about the way Luke likes my confidence and Paulina likes my smile. And maybe my body doesn't matter as much as I think it does.

Still, I have *never* been as happy with my appearance as I have been since I started taking Lipamorph. So I don't think I want to stop. But maybe I can take less of it, limit myself to one pill a week.

Maybe none of this has to be as complicated as we're all making it.

35

AMBER

I HATE THE NEWS.

I used to think I couldn't hate anything as much as I hated marketing. But then I loved Kelly from Marketing, and then she broke my heart. And *then* I realized that the news is 90% advertisements anyway. And the 10% that isn't advertisements is just TV anchors and online pseudo-journalists trying to play up controversy as much as they can, so that more people will watch or read, and they will get more ad revenue from sponsors.

I also hate the news because it tells me things I don't want to hear.

Like today, for example. It's Saturday, and Judie's busy hanging out with Luke and his super cool mom, and Kelly is God knows where, so I'm all alone once again. Lying on the couch, stuffing my face with random combinations of crunchy snacks and salty condiments, drinking cheap-ass rum right out of the bottle, and texting incoherent, borderline existentially depressed thoughts to Brianne.

I've got the TV just running in the background because there are no particular sitcoms I want to watch right now, so

I'm just letting Conventionally Attractive Blonde Anchor ramble in the background as I eat and drink my blues away.

It's not until I hear her say "Lipamorph" that she has my attention. I turn my half-drunk head toward the TV and start listening to her report.

Basically, the gist of it is this: the government is trying to decide whether or not Lipamorph deserves to be criminalized as a "drug." The way that weed still is in a lot of places, I guess. *That's not going to stop people from taking it,* is the first thought that comes to my mind.

Apparently, tons of overdoses have been reported recently.

So a new drug comes out and not everyone takes it responsibly. Big surprise.

But I guess it *is* a big surprise to some politicians. CABA interviews a few politicians who have been in the process of debating the fate of Lipamorph's continued legality. Big shocker—they're all men.

It's all men deciding the fate of a pill that's used almost exclusively by women. I almost burst out laughing at how little this surprises me.

"I hate men," I mumble to myself, suddenly recalling the time Judie burst through the front door announcing the same thing.

That's when it hits me that I'm alone in this thought now. Judie's got a fantastic boyfriend that she most definitely does not hate. And Kelly—fuck. Kelly's probably talking to Zack again or something, isn't she? The way she'd bring him up always sounded like they were on good terms.

I highly doubt Kelly hates men. In fact, she likes them quite a lot.

Then, I spend the next half hour staring at the ceiling, half-buzzed and listening to middle-aged men drone on and on about their unsolicited opinions on women's bodies.

One question is dominating my thoughts, shouting louder than all the rest: *Is this something I want to fight for?*

Last month, I was sort of fighting *against* it, in a way, with my article. But that was before the *law* got involved. Everything's different now.

Judie's always hated it when I smoke weed. It makes the apartment smell, she says. It's bad for me. Whatever else. The point is, she can hate it all she wants, but she'd never say I'm a *criminal* for using it. And as much as I hate that she wants to use Lipamorph, she doesn't deserve to be a criminal for it, either.

Plus, I can't just sit by as a group of men decide the fate of women's ability to shape their bodies. *That* goes against everything I believe as a feminist.

I didn't sit through two hours of needle penetration, resulting in a glorious "Fuck the Patriarchy" tattoo, for nothing.

"They're thinking of criminalizing Lipamorph!" I shout when I walk into our book club meeting on Friday. (Well since it's in my office, I'm technically walking back from the bathroom. But it's the first thing I say to the group.)

Rebecca sighs and drops the stack of books in her lap. I

think she's finally starting to realize that most of us aren't actually going to finish a full book. Not with all this other stuff going on.

"Thank Jesus," says Fanny. "When I heard the news, I couldn't be happier. Maybe my daughter will finally shut up about wanting to try it."

"Just because it's illegal doesn't mean she can't try it," Midge says with a raspy laugh.

Fanny looks mildly horrified at that.

"I guess you're pretty happy, huh, Amber?" asks Tanya.

I shake my head, with what I can only describe as *vigor*. "Not at all, no. I think we should fight this. Sure, I've never been a *fan* of Lipamorph, but you know what I'm *less* a fan of? Male politicians deciding what's 'best' for women. You guys should know that by now."

Kelly looks up at me. I think it's the first time she's held direct eye contact with me since our breakup.

Fanny rolls her eyes. "I'd love to get Isabelle's mother in here, and hear you say that to her face, Amber."

"Shut up, Fanny," I respond, earning an extra-mean glare from her. I'm not sure anyone ever tells Fanny to shut up. In fact, I'll bet she's one of those moms who teaches her kids that *shut up* is a swear word.

"Believe it or not, I've got a plan," I continue, looking away from Fanny. "Lipamorph wasn't the cause of Isabelle's overdose. It was a symptom of a larger problem. The only reason she even wanted to take it was so people would take her seriously. It's like Tanya was saying the other week. The real problem isn't Lipamorph—it's sexism in the workplace. So let's fight *that*."

Tanya smiles at me for the first time ever.

"I can get behind that," Samantha says from her desk. "I've been talking to Katherine a lot about this, and she's been freaking out so hard."

Katherine is Samantha's sixteen-year-old cousin, the one who probably *needs* Lipamorph more than anyone.

"So what's your plan?" asks Kelly.

I concentrate really hard on trying to slow my heart rate down. Kelly has barely talked to me since we broke up, and now she's looking right at me, and her gaze is friendly, hopeful...I might even say trusting.

"I think we just all need to utilize our own talents and create things that can't be ignored," I say. "I've been working on a *ton* of articles for *The Feminist Forum* this week. Kelly, I know they post, like, webcomics and political cartoons too. Maybe you could draw something?"

"I'd be glad to." She smiles. That smile's going to be the death of me, I swear.

"But then we can contact other sources, too. Like the Chicago news with that Conventionally Attractive Blonde Anchor we see every Saturday."

"Who?" asks Tanya. I guess most people have more interesting Saturdays than I do.

"Just...let's make stuff together," I continue. "Let's make so much stuff that we can't be ignored."

"I'm with you," says Kelly, and I almost have a heart attack.

Kelly, Samantha, Tanya, and I make plans to meet up this weekend and get some stuff done. Rebecca already has plans, which doesn't surprise me. I imagine Rebecca spends her weekends going on amazing dates with Quentin, or playing in an amateur softball league, or reading a thousand books about Chicago architecture. She probably does all of those things and more every weekend. Midge is a single mom, so we don't blame her for not being able to make it.

Fanny, though...Fanny still isn't convinced.

As I watch everyone (except Samantha) leave my tiny basement office, I hold back the urge to yell something at Fanny. I'm not sure exactly what I want to say to her. But I do want to tell her that she needs to do more for her daughter than just ban her from listening to Miz Lollipop and tell her that Lipamorph is evil. She needs to help her daughter see that her body is great the way it is.

I want to tell her that I know this from experience. That Judie and I had a mom once, too.

36

KELLY

THIS IS THE FIRST SATURDAY I'VE SPENT WITH AMBER since we broke up.

She, Tanya, Samantha, and I are all in my living room. Next to Samantha, Amber kneels on the floor in front of the coffee table, where she's placed her laptop. Tanya and I sit cross-legged on the couch, our laptops on our laps.

On the coffee table, I also have a few sketches strewn out, none in color yet.

"These are really good," Samantha mumbles, thumbing through the pile of drawings. Then she looks up at me. "Could you do a drawing to go along with an article my cousin's writing?"

"Katherine?" I ask, as if Samantha's mentioned any other cousin during our time together.

She nods. "She's been working on an essay she wants to submit somewhere. I'm not sure where she should send it yet. I'm thinking she should go big, like *New York Times* or *Huffington Post* or something, but she just thinks it'll either get rejected or get buried under the million other articles they put out each day."

That is the most words I've ever heard Samantha say in a row.

"Why doesn't she just put it on a blog?" asks Tanya. "I'm sure she could get it to go viral if we all shared it. Kelly, what do you think?" Tanya turns to me.

"I'm happy to do a drawing for her."

"Yeah, but can you also help it get tons of exposure? You're the marketing genius," says Tanya.

"I am *not* a marketing genius," I laugh, shaking my head. "Guys, I just *work* in marketing. It's really because I'm good at graphic design."

Tanya turns back to Samantha, who's once again turned her attention to my half-finished cartoons. "I'm sure we'll find a way to get Katherine's post a lot of attention," she says.

Samantha nods.

"Send me your article when you get a chance," I tell her, "and I'll get started on some art for it."

"Are there any protests planned?" Tanya asks, Googling the question on her laptop as she speaks. "If not, we should try to organize one. I'm sure with all of Rebecca's connections, we can find enough people to participate."

I'm starting to get a little overwhelmed with fighting for the continued legalization of a drug that I don't even take anymore.

"What's this?" Amber finally speaks up.

I make eye contact with her and see that she's holding up one of the half-finished drawings from the coffee table. It's a rough sketch of a girl with big eyes, light-colored hair, and a thin body inside a tailored business suit.

"It's Isabelle," I tell her. "I might give it to her as a get-well-soon present or something. I don't know."

Isabelle got released from the hospital last night but isn't allowed to return to work just yet. She's taking a week to recover at home. None of us are really sure what she looks like now, but we think she's probably pretty thin. Either way, I want her to know that I still see her as a strong, professional young woman, even if she no longer has the same body. I wasn't quite sure how to convey that feeling to her with my words, so I drew her a picture.

"It's really good," Amber says. "She's gonna love it." She pauses for a moment, then continues. "We should write an article about that."

"About Isabelle?" Tanya asks. "Isn't that kind of invasive?"

Amber shakes her head. "Not about Isabelle specifically. Just about how we need to fight sexism in the workplace because that's the real demon here."

"You should write that," I tell her. "You did a really good job on your other article."

"Was that sarcastic?" she snorts. I can't blame her. A lot of us really tore her apart for what she wrote about Judie and Lipamorph last month.

"No, it wasn't. I may have not agreed with your article, but I was being sincere. I thought you did a really good job presenting your position. You should keep writing."

Amber looks at me like she wants to smile but isn't sure if she can.

I do smile. Because even though the circumstances are horrible, I like that we're all working together for something.

And I guess it's more than that, too. It's more selfish than that, ashamed as I am to admit it.

I *like* that everyone wants me to make all these drawings for them.

Drawing pictures for Isabelle, for Katherine, for *Feminist Forum* webcomics, and *then* finishing my pieces for the upcoming art show...well, it almost makes me not want to go to work anymore. I feel like art and I just fell in love all over again.

That's when I hear a slight *thump* and turn my head to see Sienna nudging the bedroom door open. She slowly hobbles out into the living room, then stops when she sees Amber. Almost instinctively, she leaps up into Amber's lap and curls up against her, content.

37

AMBER

THE FOLLOWING WEEK, *THE FEMINIST FORUM* publishes Kelly's comic. Each panel cuts between two different women, who keep running into older men. Both ladies have great bodies, though both of them are differently proportioned. The first two panels show the men they run into trying to hit on them, with the talk bubbles saying things like, "Why do you bother to make your body so perfect if you aren't looking for attention?" Then, the next two panels show men telling them to stop taking Lipamorph because it's bad for them, and men will like their bodies regardless of whether or not they take it. Then, the final panel is one wide horizontal one across the bottom. It shows the two women coming together and kissing each other. The handwritten text at the very bottom says, "Men: It's not about you. So stay out of it."

She's gotten 50,000 views already. That's more than Alice Gilbert's gotten, and her article's been up for *months*.

After reading her comic, there is absolutely no denying it. I'm still in love with Kelly.

Luckily, I don't have too much downtime to worry about

that because Vivian Costello's still got me doing Isabelle's work until she comes back on Friday. I never thought I'd be *happy* to have to do someone else's job, but I guess avoiding your feelings does that to you.

Vivian never asks Samantha to do Isabelle's job. I guess that's because she realizes that Samantha gives a lot more of a fuck about the whole tech support thing than I do. Either that, or she forgot she has two people working in that basement. Samantha doesn't always do the best job of making her presence known.

Until recently, I mean. I'm really glad she's been sticking up for Katherine so much. Samantha sent me the first draft of Katherine's essay to read, and honestly, I almost cried. I seriously never thought a sixteen-year-old girl's writing could move me that much, but it *did.* I told Samantha that Katherine needs to send that article *everywhere* she can.

So I spend my whole day at work making photocopies that Isabelle's supposed to make, alphabetizing folders that Isabelle's supposed to organize, actively *not* thinking about Kelly, and running to the office coffee machine to make the drinks Isabelle usually does. I don't mind it. We don't have a fancy coffee maker in the basement room, obviously, so I enjoy getting to play with all the different latte settings. I guess I can see why Judie likes working at Big Mama's so much.

I've learned that Vivian and I both enjoy a good double-shot mocha with extra foam.

"I'd like it better with a third shot," Vivian says, taking a sip from the fancy Costello's Accounting mug I hand to her. "A shot of rum."

"I feel you, Vivian," I answer, taking a sip of mine in return. "I'd like mine better if *both* of the shots were rum."

"Cheers to that," says Vivian, and then we clink our mugs together.

Vivian Costello's really not that scary, once you get to know her. I guess that's something I'm realizing more and more about people in general, as I get to know them all better—that they're often *really* different from our first impressions of them.

Vivian's just powerful. She's confident, and commanding, and no-nonsense about her company. But she's the president of the whole operation, so that makes sense. Vivian the *person*, though—the Vivian it feels okay to call by just her first name—she's just a person like the rest of us.

That becomes even clearer to me that evening.

I'm on the Purple Line, almost at the Merchandise Mart stop, which gets me thinking about Kelly's upcoming art show again. So I reach for my phone in my pocket, so I can just look at some goofy pictures of puppies or something and keep my mind off of Kelly. But my phone's not there.

I almost literally smack myself in the forehead when I remember that I left it on the main floor of Costello's along with the earbuds I was using to listen to music while I made photocopies.

So I get off at the Merchandise Mart, run up the stairs and down over to the other side of the platform, and get on the Brown Line back into the Loop.

When I reach Costello's, it's almost six in the evening, and since it's already late fall, the sky is pitch black. Almost everyone's heading out for the day, so I run into our building and rush to our suite.

I find my phone sitting on the copy machine, just like I expected. No one even moved it or anything. So I grab my phone, wrap the cord to my earbuds around it, and shove it in my back pocket. I turn to head out, but I hear a noise that drives me to a halt.

It's like...heavy breathing, mixed with whimpers. Coming out of Vivian's office.

Maybe it's the lighthearted rapport that she and I have built lately, or maybe it's just life without Kelly making me even more apathetic than usual, but I don't even hesitate. I just knock on Vivian's door.

"Just a second," her muffled voice comes from the other end.

When she opens the door, my heart stops for a second. I take her all in, standing there in front of me, with puffy pinkish bags under her eyes, and small tracks of black mascara dotting her cheeks.

"Oh, hi, Amber," she says. "What's going on?"

"Um. I...I just...well, I left my phone here, and then when I came back to get it, I heard something coming from your office, and I just wanted—I wanted to check...you know, that you were okay and everything."

She forces a small smile onto her face. "Oh, everything is okay. You don't need to worry," she says.

If this were a month ago, I would've left it at that, and

bolted out of there. Well, actually, if it were a month ago, I wouldn't have been brave enough to knock on Vivian's door in the first place. But I guess, even after our breakup, Kelly's still managed to awaken something fearless in me. Something that can see a person as more than the confidence she exudes.

"Do...do you want to talk about it, or anything?"

She just stares at me for a moment, and at first I'm worried that she's insulted that the tech support girl even imagines that the CEO would ever deign to confide in her.

But then she gestures for me to come inside her office. I walk in, and she closes the door behind me. She gestures to a chair across from her giant mahogany desk. I sit down.

"You've been doing a really good job, Amber," she starts. "I really do appreciate you taking on Isabelle's workload while she's been out. Earlier today, I realized I'd forgotten to thank you for that."

"Oh, it's—it's no problem at all. I'm happy to help." Honestly, it had never even occurred to me that Vivian Costello would ever thank me for *anything*.

"Times are weird right now, aren't they?"

I almost laugh at that. It's the understatement of the decade. "They sure are."

"The divorce has been really hard on me," she says. "My husband and I—I don't know. It was a long time coming. We just weren't right for each other."

"I'm sorry to hear about your divorce." I didn't even know that she was married. Her personal life had always been this big mystery-slash-fantasy.

She nods and wipes her eyes with a tissue. "Thank you. I'm not really sad about losing *him*, though. I've been around long enough to know when two people just don't fit together. It's more about the *stress*. All the legal procedures. All the *paperwork*. That probably sounds ridiculous, right?" She laughs a little. "I mean, for God's sake, I'm an *accountant*!"

Until now, I'd never heard Vivian Costello laugh. I hadn't even fantasized about it. It just wasn't a thought that had ever crossed my mind.

And then...then, I have no idea where this confidence comes from—maybe my coffee *did* have a mystery rum shot in it after all, or maybe my nonexistent filter doesn't care that it's Vivian I'm talking to—but I just say what's on my mind. "Did you love him?"

I immediately feel a little tinge of regret, like maybe I shouldn't be asking my *boss* these super personal questions.

But she just nods softly. "I did, for a while. Love can fade. Sometimes it just wasn't meant to work out. And the older you get, the more you learn that's okay."

I let out a heavy sigh, briefly embarrassed at how loud it must have sounded. But I can't help it...she got me thinking about *Kelly* again. Fucking Kelly. (It hurts more than *Fucking Lindsey*.)

And I'm wondering if maybe she's one of those people I'm just not meant to work out with, and if I should grow up and accept it like Vivian has.

Then I make contact with Vivian's bloodshot eyes. Chocolate brown, with red veins circling the irises, and tracks of black mascara underneath. A month ago, I would've thought those eyes could've shot lasers directly through me. And it hits me, that this gorgeous, powerful, terrifying woman, whom I'd spent *years* living in fear of, is *not afraid* to be completely emotionally vulnerable in front of me.

It's then that I realize that Vivian's meant to teach me a very different kind of lesson.

38

JUDIE

When Paulina leaves to go back to Greece, I feel a ton of different emotions at once. At the forefront, of course, is sadness. I don't *want* to see Paulina go. I'd love to have her working at Big Mama's with us every day for the rest of my life. At the same time, I feel super happy because I'm glad I met her. I feel like Paulina's given me a completely different perspective on myself and my own body image. Finally, I feel jealousy. Jealousy toward Luke. Luke got to live his whole life with this super cool, super sweet, amazing mom, and I had to live with parents that constantly saw me and Amber as disappointments. In a way, I kind of feel like Paulina could be my mom. Not *literally*, of course. Because then Luke would be my brother, which would mean I couldn't date him. I just mean that she could be a mother figure to me. A replacement mom since the first one I got was defective.

I don't have a *ton* of time to spend missing Paulina because Amber immediately starts demanding my time. In a good way, I mean.

She's recruited me to help her with the effort she and some of the girls from her book club are making to help keep Lipamorph legal. Next week, the government's planning to vote on whether or not it should remain legal to use without a doctor's prescription, at least in Illinois. (Because, when the federal government can't decide on something, it seems like their default position is just "leave it to the states.")

Of course I want to help her with this. Even though Paulina inspired me to love my body regardless of how it looks, I still do want to take Lipamorph here and there. I'm capable of taking it responsibly. Miz Lollipop may still be my favorite musician, but I'll never look to her, or Betty J or Ella Esmeralda or any of them, when it comes to health advice.

I'm glad Amber's fighting for this. It actually surprised me when I found out she was.

"I thought you hated Lipamorph," was the first thing I said to her, after she'd asked me to join with her.

"I do," she'd said, "but it doesn't matter if I hate it. I support your right to do whatever the fuck you want. Much more than I support some random politician's right to *tell* you whatever the fuck *he* wants you to do."

That was probably one of the sweetest moments we'd ever shared as sisters. Even sweeter than the time we cried at prom together in our high-school bathroom.

So me, Amber, Kelly, and a few other girls from her book club are planning this demonstration we're going to put on at the Merchandise Mart during Kelly's big art show this weekend.

Apparently, one of our senators, John DuMont, is going to be at the art show. He RSVP'd "Going" to the Facebook event for this show, and to a few of the evites online. He's been pretty vocal about Lipamorph being unhealthy, and that it should be classified as a drug like heroin or meth or something. Most recently, he went under fire for going on the news and referring to the ladies who use Lipamorph as "disproportionate bimbos."

He had this big spread in the *Chicago Tribune* where he talked all about how Lipamorph is unhealthy and immoral, and adds to an oversexualized society. There was this art that went along with it, which showed a bunch of ladies with huge boobs saying stuff like, "My eyes are down here," and "I've got more in my chest than in my head."

Honestly, it was like something straight out of the 1960s. And not in a cool, vintage aesthetic way either.

According to Amber, Kelly's planning an art display that's going to go against this somehow. And we're all supposed to individually approach John DuMont and tell him, face-to-face, why we're not disproportionate bimbos.

I'm not sure how I feel about confronting a high-powered politician and telling him that I'm smart and worthy of respect and all that. Partially because, until recently, I didn't even believe that myself.

Amber also says that she doubts it'll be long before John DuMont's caught on tape in some kind of extramarital affair with one of those "disproportionate bimbos" he claims to hate so much.

On Friday evening, the night before the art show,

Amber and I are just chilling on our couch like always. *Friends* is playing in the background, and Amber's shoveling handfuls of buffalo-sauce-drenched Fritos into her mouth. I'm sitting next to her, sipping at my rum and Coke, and thinking about everything that's happened these past few months.

"Amber."

She turns her head to face me, sticking her tongue out to lick the remnants of buffalo sauce around her mouth. "What's up?"

"If you want to, you know, smoke in here, go ahead."

She blinks. "Yeah. I was planning on it later. Why?"

"I just mean...I'm sorry I called you a pot head so much. I don't mind it anymore. Like, I don't ever want to smoke weed, but if you want to, I won't judge you for it anymore."

Her eyes widen a little. I don't think she was expecting that. "But I thought you didn't like *drugs*, Judie?" A goofy little smile starts playing on her lips. I know she's trying to get my goat.

"Well, you're helping me fight to keep the drug I use legal. So the least I can do is stop judging *you* for what you do to your own body."

She bursts out laughing then, and even slaps the armrest of the couch for effect. "Oh man, Judie! I never thought this day would come!"

I shrug. "Well, it has."

I would be delusional not to recognize Lipamorph as a drug by now. Especially after what happened to Miz

Lollipop. And to Amber's friend Isabelle. So I guess Amber and I are both drug users, in our own way.

It's just another one of those weird sister connections.

39

KELLY

Two hours before the art show starts, I'm nervous as hell. This is an entirely new feeling. Art is one thing that's *never* made me nervous. It's always relaxed me. Art was the number one thing that helped me feel comfortable being myself.

But that was before my art was going to be on display for everyone's judgment. That was before I was using my art for a political cause. That was before I had an ex-girlfriend who would be here looking at my art, and thinking about the ways the concepts I'm going to show led to our breakup. That was back when I was doing watercolor portraits of Sienna for my own gratification, or doodles in coffee stains on napkins to impress a quirky professor.

That was before I realized I want to do art as a career.

I know, it's irresponsible. Artists make almost no money. My bank account's always been the one thing I've never had to worry about. If I decide to pursue art full-time, God knows I won't be able to afford a two-bedroom apartment in Lakeview by myself anymore. But I could have a roommate. I have *friends* now.

I've got my display all set up inside one of the ground-floor Merchandise Mart showrooms.

Standing on three white blocks are my sculptures of the girls I saw outside West Loop College, with the bobblehead girl in the middle. They're right at the start of the display, right under my name.

Next, on the wall behind them, is my big canvas oil painting of Jessica from Page 14. She's in bright neon colors with a thick black outline, like a pop-art comic. Her skin, eyes, and lips are made of tiny circular dots, Lichtenstein-style. Instead of page 14 of *Playboy*, I've placed Jessica on the cover of a fictitious magazine I've titled *Sculpt Yourself*. The title is displayed proudly across the top in shaded block letters, colored in with the same dots I used on Jessica's body.

If Finnegan & Peters accuses me of treason, or intellectual property theft, or hurt feelings because I appropriated their slogan, well...I don't really care anymore.

Next to that painting, I have a large, blown-up version of my *Feminist Forum* comic, framed in black with a shiny glass covering.

After that is my photography display.

Over the past week, I met up with my subjects after work, and did portraits of them against the blank white wall of my second-bedroom studio. I set up some clamp lamps from ACE Hardware around the room, and turned one on at a time, creating a heavy shadow contrast and a dramatic chiaroscuro effect. Kind of like the dramatic blonde lady in the very first Lipamorph commercial. Maybe Finnegan &

Peters will be upset with me about that, too. Again, I don't really care.

The first portrait is of Isabelle. After she got out of the hospital, Isabelle was definitely thin, but she wasn't a borderline spectacle of body horror like Miz Lollipop. The fat started traveling from her boobs to her upper arms. It would just go there without warning, and there was nothing she could do to stop it. She went to the hospital pretty much as soon as she noticed the fat going wherever it wanted. Since they caught it early enough, she thankfully didn't have to get anything amputated. But she does have a giant, violent-looking scar on each bicep from the incision they made to remove the excess fat.

"I'm thinking I might get some kind of tattoos to cover the scars," Isabelle told me when she was at my apartment this past week.

I almost laughed at that; picturing adorable little Isabelle with some tough-girl "Fuck the Patriarchy" tattoo like Amber has. But I didn't laugh because, in a way, people not taking Isabelle seriously was kind of what got her into this mess in the first place.

For the photo-shoot, Isabelle wore a dark-grey, professional-looking A-line skirt, and a collared, button-down white blouse. Short-sleeved, of course, so her scars were visible.

On the wall of the Merchandise Mart, Isabelle's photo hangs in black and white, except for her scars, which I've made a striking shade of dark red. Just like Blonde Lady's lipstick was in the first Lipamorph commercial.

In a way, I guess my art display kind of pokes fun at the whole business of marketing, too.

The other person I photographed was Katherine.

Samantha got Katherine to come to Chicago to visit her last weekend. Katherine ended up posting her essay on Medium, and it got a couple thousand shares. Samantha, Tanya, Amber, Judie, and I each emailed it to Senator John DuMont, too.

In Katherine's photo, she's wearing her school uniform: a white polo and waist-high navy pleated skirt. Below her collar, *George Washington High School* is embroidered. I also made her photo black-and-white, except for the embroidery of her school name, which I made the same red as Isabelle's scars.

I want to make sure that *everyone* looking at this photo knows that Katherine is just a kid.

Their photos, printed on 16-by-24, portrait-oriented canvases, hang next to each other on the wall. Underneath them, I've printed the title of the piece in black typewriter font: *Disproportionate Bimbos.*

I hope to God that John DuMont understands the concept of irony, or at the very least, sarcasm.

On the wall, hanging over my entire display, is a plank of wood with giant block letters nailed to it, announcing the name of the whole collection: *We're All Just Works of Art.*

After checking that everything's in order on my display, I try to mentally prepare myself for people arriving. I do some slow, in-and-out yoga breaths that Rebecca taught me, hoping to slow my heart rate.

The first person to show up is Zack.

Well, first *two* people, I guess since he's brought Heather with him.

I immediately abandon my art display, and run up to give him a big hug. "Zack! I can't believe you came!"

He smiles. "Of course. Heather and I had been meaning to visit Chicago at some point anyway, so I figured, why not come and see the work of our favorite artist?"

Heather extends her hand. "I'm Heather," she says. "It's nice to meet you."

I shake her hand, but I still can't get over the way Zack said *our* favorite artist. Like Heather's been looking at photos of my art with Zack and agreeing that it's good, or something. Like Heather's the kind of girl who enjoys spending an afternoon looking at her boyfriend's ex-girlfriend's art. Then I remember that Heather's dad is a therapist, and that she knows how to maturely handle relationships better than probably anyone else in the world.

I could even see myself being invited to Zack and Heather's wedding in a few years or something. Even being in the wedding party. *Why can't everyone approach relationships this way*, I wonder.

Arriving next is Samantha, who's brought Katherine with her.

Samantha greets me, while Katherine immediately makes a beeline for the photo display of her and Isabelle.

"I didn't know Katherine was coming back to Chicago this weekend," I tell her.

Samantha nods. "She really wanted to see the photo of

her on display. She also really liked Chicago. I think she's gonna look at some colleges here."

Then Katherine runs back from the photos and taps me on the shoulder. "Kelly!" she shouts and wraps her arms around me in a hug. "I love it. It looks so good!" she tells my sleeve.

"Aw. Thank you so much." I break away from the hug, and look Katherine in the eyes. "Your essay was *so* good, too. Thanks for writing it."

Then, she gives me a high-five and runs back to the photo display to look at it some more.

Samantha laughs quietly. "You're all she talks about, you know," she says. "I think you're her new role model."

At first, I furrow my eyebrows a little bit at that. I'm not sure I can handle being someone's role model. I can barely live up to the expectations my significant others set for me. But the more I think about it, I guess it's okay. Katherine's just a kid, and if having a twenty-four-year-old artist to look up to makes her happy, then who am I to stop her?

Isabelle shows up soon after, and she and Katherine spend a lot of the night looking at their photos together. Then Tanya arrives, and she goes crazy over my Lichtenstein-style rendition of Jessica from Page 14.

Rebecca and Quentin stop by, too. "I can't believe you're in a *Merchandise Mart showroom*, Kelly!" Rebecca squeals, hugging me.

Until I'd applied to feature my art at this show, I didn't even know that Merchandise Mart showrooms were such a big deal. But Rebecca probably has a whole encyclopedia in her head about the history and architecture and cultural significance of the Merchandise Mart, so I decide to feel her excitement through osmosis.

Finally, Amber and Judie get there, along with Luke. Judie looks stylish, as usual. Her body still has the proportions I know she achieved through Lipamorph, but they're slightly less intense. I think Judie's trying to take it in moderation. Maybe I'll try that at some point, too. I don't know. Right now, I'm pretty happy without it.

Amber looks great, too.

She's not wearing one of her baggy hoodies like usual. Instead, she's wearing an open button-down plaid shirt, with one of her black 2000s emo-phase T-shirts underneath. She's got brown boots on over her skinny jeans, rather than her usual beat-up black Converses. It's similar to how she dressed on our first date. She's even got her hair down.

I wonder if Judie convinced her to dress nice for this. I can easily picture it in my head: Judie grabbing Amber by the shoulders and steering her toward her bedroom closet, forcing her to pick out something just a little nicer than usual for an art show.

I also wonder if Amber decided on her own that she wanted to look nice for this show. For me, even.

Fanny Spitzer never shows up.

Neither does Senator John DuMont. What a shock; a politician doesn't keep his promise.

So maybe my art show isn't going to have as much influence on the vote over Lipamorph as I was hoping it would. But as I look around the room, I'm not disappointed.

I watch Rebecca and Quentin gawking at my sculptures. I see Tanya studying the color in my painting of Jessica from Page 14. I watch Isabelle and Katherine's budding friendship, as they excitedly talk to each other about the photos they modeled for. And I realize that my art *does* have influence. It has meaning for a lot of people.

Maybe Zack was right. Maybe it's not just that other people think I'm cooler than I am. Maybe I'm also cooler than I realize.

"Hey."

I turn my head to see Amber standing next to me. She's holding a paper plate full of hors d'oeuvres from the lobby. I should've known Amber would take the first opportunity she could to find food. Her plate is piled high with grapes, crackers, and hummus. You know, standard reception food. She never even complains once about a lack of potato chips or barbecue sauces. She just stands next to me, shoving healthy food into her mouth, and staring at my art.

"Hi, Amber." I smile at her. "Your hair looks nice down."

She nods and swallows the grape in her mouth. "Thanks. Your art is fantastic."

"Thanks."

We stay silent for a moment as Amber stuffs her face with crackers. She swallows. "Why are you working in marketing, again?"

I take a deep breath. It's time for a thought I hadn't yet vocalized. "I'm not sure if I'm going to do that forever. I want to start spending more time on this." I gesture to all the art in front of me.

A giant smile takes over Amber's face, and she nods.

Then she cocks her head, and gestures with her hand for me to follow her. She starts walking toward my display, and I walk behind her.

She stops in front of one of the pieces at the end of my display.

"Okay, so I get this art display as a whole," she says. "I get the whole 'We're All Just Works of Art' thing. I get the sculptures of the girls from my college, and the photos of Isabelle and Katherine and the way you sarcastically call out John DuMont's sexist language. I get the pop-art *Playboy* model thing, and obviously I get *the Feminist Forum* comic."

I nod. "I'm glad it's all fitting together."

"Well," she continues. "It doesn't. I don't get how this piece ties in to your overall message."

She points to the last picture in my display. All the way at the end, smaller than the rest of the pieces. It does seem out of place. It's a watercolor painting of Amber sitting on my green armchair with Sienna in her lap. I made it from the sketch I did of her that day a few months ago, when she posed for me.

A small smile creeps onto my lips, and I almost let a tiny giggle escape. "I guess it doesn't," I tell her. "It doesn't really fit with everything else."

She looks at me. "Then why did you include it?"

"Well, I—you know, I just like it."

40

AMBER

It's Monday in the basement of Costello's again. Once again, I have next to no work to do because Isabelle's back at work now.

At Kelly's art show on Saturday night, I talked to Isabelle. I told her that she should set up a meeting with Vivian Costello about how she wants to be taken more seriously at work. She seemed a little scared at first—which, I don't blame her for; being an intern is *hard*—but I explained to her how I got to know Vivian over the last couple weeks, and how she's not half as scary as we initially thought. I think she's going to take my advice.

Then, Kelly, Tanya, Samantha, Judie, and I spent Sunday calling various Illinois senators and asking them to please vote to keep Lipamorph legal. Even if it needs to be better regulated or something, we said. Even if you need to put out warnings on it.

They'll be voting later this week. Judie and Samantha are super nervous, but I think we've done all we can reasonably do at this point.

So I'm just spinning around in my chair again like usual, drinking one of the nice coffees from the machine I've learned we have upstairs, and listening to a YouTube playlist. Today, I'm actually listening to a Miz Lollipop playlist. I'm still not a fan of her, but Judie made me a mix of some of her songs that she specifically thought I'd like, so I've decided to give her a chance. So far, I'm still not convinced, but I'm only three songs in, so I'll keep listening for a bit.

One thing keeps gnawing at me. I keep remembering how last week, Vivian Costello opened up to me, how she let me see her while she was emotionally vulnerable. How she never once lost the respect I have for her, even though I basically saw her cry over her divorce.

And that gets me to thinking about how we can be strong, but still allow ourselves to show emotions and to be vulnerable.

I guess Kelly kind of did that at her art display this past weekend. She put all her art out there for the world (or, I guess, most of Chicago) to see—art that showed her opinions and her desires. I can't help it; I keep fixating on that picture she had at the end of me with Sienna on my lap. She didn't need to include that picture. It really had no relevance to the rest of the display.

But she put it there. Because she liked it.

I think it's time for me to put my emotions on the line, too.

So I pull my phone out of my back pocket and text Kelly

to meet me in our bathroom once she has a chance because I want to talk. I phrase it like that: *our* bathroom. *Go big or go home*, I tell myself.

Twenty minutes later, we're standing in the basement bathroom together. Not in a stall or anything, just next to the sink. Where we met, sort of.

"What did you want to talk about?" she asks.

I take a deep breath, feeling my elevated heart rate thumping in my throat. Then I spit it out. "I'm still in love with you."

Her eyes widen. I can't even begin to try reading the expression on her face. Is she excited? Scared? Happy? I have literally no idea.

So I just continue talking. "I don't know if you're interested, but if you are, I really want to try again. I've learned the only way to show who you really are to other people is to be direct, and to open yourself up emotionally. So I'm just going to lay it all out there. I've never been as happy as I've been with you. I don't care if you're not the exact person I first imagined you were. You're the only person I've ever met who wants to make out with me in a bathroom stall, or eat barbecue-sauced covered chips at an abandoned train stop, or spend all Saturday playing drinking games to overrated sitcom reruns with me. Other than my sister, I mean. You're the only person I want to *date* who does all those things—"

I'm starting to ramble, but thankfully, Kelly shuts me up. She shuts me up *really* quick when her face lunges forward, and our lips collide.

When we break away from the kiss, we just stand there for a few minutes, smiling, unsure of what to say next.

"I just want to make sure we go into it with complete honesty this time," I tell her.

She nods. "I agree. We need to communicate better. Let's start now."

"Right. No secrets this time."

"None."

I kiss her cheek. "Do you want to play truth or dare again? Or maybe, like, a more efficient version of it, where we just start over and tell each other everything?"

"Yeah."

"Okay." I take a deep breath. "We'll call this Truth Game. Introduce yourself to me, and tell me everything. I don't care how embarrassing, or controversial, or risky."

She extends her hand, and I shake it.

"Hi, I'm Kelly from Marketing," she says, "and I once fell asleep on the toilet."

I laugh. Kelly's got the idea. "Hi, I'm Amber from Tech Support," I reply, "and freshman year of college, I threw up during my Intro to Social Policy final. That's how I learned my limits when it came to rum and Coke."

"Hi, I'm Kelly the Artist," she continues, "and back in college, I regularly drew *Harry Potter* porn."

"Hi, I'm Amber the Angry Feminist, and when *I* was in college, I had sex with my best friend and roommate."

"Hi, I'm Kelly, and I'm still good friends with my ex-boyfriend, and I plan to keep it that way, even though I no longer have any feelings for him."

"I'm Amber, and I love your body. No matter how you create it. The way it is now, the way it was when you used Lipamorph, the way it's going to look when we're saggy-skinned ninety-year-olds. I don't care. I love your body."

"I'm Kelly," she says, breaking out into a huge smile. "And I *love* your freckles."

INTERESTED IN MORE BY SAVY LEISER?

Check out a preview of *The Making of A Small-Town Beauty King*.

ONE

SUNDAY

Hard work. Hard work and just being a nice guy. Isn't that what it's all about? Also, the hokey pokey. Scratch. *I first learned the value of hard work at a young age. Six, when I earned my first dollar. It was for unclogging my grandpa's toilet. Looking back, I was undervaluing my services.* Scratch.

Jackie Almond sighed and crossed out another line of writing in his notebook. Underneath the "College Essay" heading at the top, the entire page was covered in the dark blue ink of words crossed out. It was less than an hour until closing at Almond's Convenience Store, which meant Jackie could take his focus away from the overwhelming lack of customers in front of him at the cash register, and instead put his focus on his overwhelming lack of college essay topics.

Self-reflection. Something I first truly experienced after reading The Catcher in the Rye. *What a book. I was never the same.* SCRATCH.

"Excuse me, son?" A low, rumbly voice penetrated Jackie's concentration, not that he minded. He looked up to see an obese, balding man with an abundance of arm hair and a lime-green polo tucked into his khakis standing before him. This, plus his wimpy comb-over and overpowering scent of discount cologne all combined to make him exactly the type of customer Jackie was expecting. "I'd like to buy one of these." Jackie watched as the man placed a copy of the *Grey Acres Gazette* on the counter. The front-page headline, "94th Annual Town Fair Comes to Grey Acres," stared up at him.

"Fifty cents. Anything else?"

He stared straight into Jackie's eyes. "Well, you know, I *wanted* a sandwich from the deli." A moment of silence slowly passed, the man never breaking eye contact.

Jackie drew a deep breath, preparing himself for the argument he knew was coming. There was one almost every shift. "I'm sorry, sir. The deli closes at nine."

"I *know* the deli closes at nine. Why don't you think I have a sandwich?" The man even cocked his head a little for dramatic effect.

"Oh, uh, I'm sorry—"

"People are still hungry after nine, you know. The human body doesn't magically stop metabolizing just because it's nine o'clock." His hands gestured wildly, especially around the word "magically."

Jackie blinked. "I understand that. That's why we've got snacks, you know, like chips and stuff—"

"I don't want chips and stuff. I want a sandwich."

Jackie stared at the man for a moment. He blinked again. "The newspaper's fifty cents."

Ten p.m. couldn't come fast enough. After the man strutted out of the store, frustratedly swinging the newspaper at his side, Jackie spent the rest of the hour dividing his attention between his nonexistent college essay and the second hand of his watch. As soon as ten o'clock hit, Jackie started unpinning his nametag, his jittery fingers fumbling with the same rush of excitement he felt every night.

"It's ten, Dad!" Jackie shouted from the register.

His father, Jack Almond Sr., poked his head out from the Employees Only door, his hair greasy with Rogaine and a hard day's work. "Flip the sign on your way out," he called.

Jackie stuffed his nametag in his pocket and headed for the door, flipping the hanging sign to the "Closed" side on his way out and pulling his cell phone out of his jeans pocket. After sending a quick text to his best friend, Logan Feinstein, saying that he'd be on the roof in just a sec, he walked out the door, past the neon-red flickering "Convenience Store" sign, and over to a ladder on the side of the building.

He climbed the ladder until he reached the roof, where he found Logan waiting for him the same way he was every night: lying on his back, holding some sort of reading material above his head. Tonight, it was the *Grey Acres Gazette*.

The roof of Almond's Convenience Store had been

Jackie and Logan's special meeting place ever since Jackie had started working there about two years ago, the day after his sixteenth birthday. Sixteen was the legal working age in Grey Acres, but Jack Sr. thought it would be rude to request that Jackie start working *on* his birthday, so he waited until the day after to employ him. Of course, he couldn't resist giving Jackie his convenience store nametag in a Fine Jewelry box as one of his birthday gifts. Jackie found the gag a weird mix of kinda-funny and kinda-frustrating. It was like the feeling he got when he ate mediocre pizza or dark chocolate. A little pleasure with a little disappointment.

Maybe the nametag in a gift box is a metaphor for my life, thought Jackie, before filing it away in his brain as a possible college essay topic, then taking a seat cross-legged on the roof next to Logan.

"Did you see the headline on page three?" Logan asked, rocking his body forward to sit up.

"I've started actively avoiding reading the newspapers at this point," said Jackie.

"'Local Grey Acres Woman Teaches Cat to Fertilize Mushrooms.' Fascinating."

"And to think. Every other customer who came in today will be reading this story tonight."

"You think the cat shits on the mushrooms himself, or what?"

Jackie shrugged, nodding.

Jackie and Logan had been best friends since before kindergarten. Back in the early 2000s, Jack Almond Sr. and Logan's dad, Ronald Feinstein, would go to meetings of the

Midwest Small Business Owners' Society together, Jack for his convenience store and Ronald for his department store at the Grey Acres Mall. Because of that, the two of them were always meeting up for lunch to discuss their businesses, or "talk shop" as they called it, and sometimes brought little Jackie and little Logan along with them. Jackie and Logan would spend those afternoons crawling under tables at restaurants or drawing on tablecloths in crayon, whispering to each other about how "talking shop makes daddies boring."

Of course, this meant that when Jackie and Logan started school at Grey Acres Elementary, they already had each other as a best friend, and it just kind of naturally stayed that way.

"Speaking of breaking news," said Logan, his voice muffled by a loud rustling as he turned a page in the newspaper, "I heard through the grapevine that Erin's planning to ask me out to the Town Fair this Saturday."

"Oooh. Logan's got a daaaate."

"To the *fair*. It's like, 'Ooh, look at this award-winning tomato, honey. It's red and juicy just like my heart. And this second-place pumpkin is round and firm like your body.' How romantic."

"*Second*-place pumpkin?"

Logan's eyes didn't look up from the newspaper. "I'm aiming low to avoid disappointment. Besides, who even brings dates to the fair anymore? I should be like, 'Hey, Erin. 1962 called. It wants to ask you on a date to the fair.'"

Back in middle school, Jackie and Logan were the infamous duo who took girls out on double dates together, usually to a school dance or the Grey Acres Mall, and usually breaking it off after one or two dates. It wasn't their fault, though; Grey Acres Junior High dances and the Grey Acres Mall were, for the most part, barren, pathetic date spots. Not even a Shakespearean couple could fall in love there, unless they were a Shakespearean couple with a fetish for places that hadn't been renovated since the early 80s. Jackie and Logan managed to keep this routine up through the beginning of their sophomore year of high school when, out of nowhere, Logan started to show a sharp decline in his interest in girls, and a sharp, *sharp* increase in his interest in books. Jackie thought this was kinda lame at first, but within a few months, he had a job at his dad's store thrust upon him, and his dating life saw an unintentional plummet as well. Yet, even when both of them had both time and an interested pair of girls on their side, Logan showed little to no interest, which disappointed Jackie until he found out why.

Jackie chuckled at Logan's produce analogy. "We're talking about Aaron here, right? Tall Aaron who always wears those funky little bow ties?"

"Nope. Erin with an E."

"Oh. Sorry, bud."

Logan sighed. "Like I'd get a date with Aaron with an A. That'd be the day, right?"

"I dunno," Jackie said, shrugging. "Anything's possible."

"Grey Acres isn't ready for that kinda thing yet."

"Grey Acres is still fascinated by a cat taking a dump on fungus. I really wouldn't take it personally."

Logan laughed. "Yeah, I guess you're right."

A moment of silence followed, leaving Jackie and Logan looking out at the town of Grey Acres, or as much of it as they could see from a one-story convenience store roof. Past the store's parking lot stretched a few acres of empty grass that no one ever bothered to use for their intended agricultural purposes. In just six days, the annual Town Fair would be set up there, turning an empty field of crunchy, puke-colored, brownish-green grass into an elaborate setup of white tents and wooden stages. Off in the distance, they could see the faint outline of Grey Acres High School, lit up by the street lamps around it. To their left, they saw the town's only notable restaurant, a combination Crunchy's Chicken and Paul's Pancake World, as well as a dimly lit Gus's Supermarket. Logan was always annoyed that the supermarket's owner, Gus Bennett, didn't name the store Gus's Groceries. It was a painful waste of alliteration, and Logan knew that, if it weren't the only grocery store in town, Gus would be missing out on some serious marketing opportunities. To their right, Jackie and Logan saw a few houses haphazardly placed throughout the fields, without any real order or system. Jackie always theorized that John Greyacres, or whatever the original Grey Acres city planner's name was, just decided to vomit all over a giant piece of paper, and wherever the biggest chunks landed, that's where he put houses. It made more sense than any other system. The house with the largest field around it held Simon's

Pumpkin Farm, the family-owned pumpkin business that dominated the produce-growing competitions at the fair every year. Jackie and Logan both sighed. Trying to take in all of Grey Acres at once always proved disappointing.

"Man, I am *so* glad I'm getting out of this town," said Logan. "I submitted six more applications today. Last month was NYU and UCLA, and then today was UChicago, USC—"

"Oh *shit*!" Jackie snapped out of his trance. "I totally forgot. I gotta meet with *Flounder* tomorrow."

TWO

MONDAY

Jackie sat slumped over in his chair, rhythmically drumming his fingers on his knees. Every few seconds, he looked up to see his guidance counselor, Marvin Flounder, sorting through the mountain of manila folders on his desk, stopping every so often to inhale with an obnoxious *snort*. Marvin Flounder was the kind of man who proudly sported a balding head with pre-cancerous sunspots, a bushy black mustache, and Coke-bottle glasses, and who treated motivational posters from Target as if they were wallpaper. Jackie's eyes darted to the poster placed directly behind Flounder's desk, which featured a neon-yellow smiley face surrounded by a circle of Comic Sans text: "Shoot for the moon! If you miss, you might just land in Mr. Flounder's office!"

"Jackson Almond!" Flounder's painfully nasal voice boomed, as he slammed a manila folder down on top of his folder mountain.

"You know I go by Jackie, right?"

"Yes, Jackson, but this morning I read in a poll that most colleges dislike gender neutral names. I'm doing you a favor."

"Well, then I'd hate to be a Jamie. Or a Taylor. Or James Taylor. Not because of the name, just because his music's kinda boring."

Flounder made a dramatic show of rolling his eyes, so much that his head even rolled around a little bit. He then opened Jackie's manila folder and flipped through the pages. "Cornell, I see? And with Michigan as your second choice. I guess we're aiming high, aren't we, Jackson? Shooting for the *moooooon*?"

Jackie watched the little black eyes on the smiley face above Flounder's desk as they stared into his soul. "Well, yeah. I mean, I'm gonna be the first one in my family to go to college, so I figured, might as well go all out."

"Mmmm *hmmmmm*," Flounder's piercingly nasal voice vibrated. "And what is it you're planning to study?"

"I mean, I guess I've always liked a little of everything," Jackie said, shrugging. "Maybe start off with some history, have a little English, some math on the side. You know, like a big educational buffet."

"*Interesting*. I thought that spending so much time with that Logan Feinstein would have given you some focus. I received notice that, so far, he's applied to eight English programs, *three* of them Ivies."

"Isn't it like, illegal for you to reveal that information or something? Like, isn't there some sort of counselor-student confidentiality clause?"

Flounder rolled his eyes again, this time punctuating his eye-roll with one of his *snorts*. "I'm being *serious,* Jackson."

Jackie, who had been being serious as well, took a moment to appreciate that he'd never felt any desire to share any of his personal problems with Flounder.

"So," Flounder continued, "*No* idea what you want to study? At *all*?"

"I mean..." Jackie looked around the room, hoping a motivational poster might give him the answer Flounder wanted. "I guess not. Isn't part of college, like, finding yourself? Learning your 'purpose' and all that existential stuff?"

"Look, you don't seem to get it, so I'll just give it to you straight. Your grades are good... ish. Your SAT is *slightly* above average, but without a passion, or without something you excel at, what's setting you apart from every other competent kid that applies? Nothing, Jackson. You have *nothing.*"

Jackie froze for a moment, realizing he'd never been given anything that straight before. He always knew he wasn't quite as smart as Logan, but then again, most kids weren't. He was used to regular compliments from his dad on his work ethic, including a few employee-of-the-month awards at the convenience store, which he was promised every time were free of nepotism. But, it was turning out, most college-bound kids were hard workers. "I guess I could have my essay," Jackie finally answered. "I'd stand out to them if I wrote a really kick-ass essay, right?"

Flounder glared at Jackie and pointed to a motivational poster hanging on the wall to Jackie's left. It featured a fuzzy brown teddy bear with a bar of soap jammed in its mouth, accompanied by text reading, "Watch your language, kids."

"A kick... rear-end essay?" Jackie offered.

"Very good. Now, what do you plan to write about?"

Jackie reviewed his list of failed essay topics from the night before. There was only one he hadn't yet attempted. "Well, I was thinking, how about my dad, Jack Almond Sr.? Great guy. Grew up in poverty, beat cancer twice, eventually achieved his goal of owning his own convenience store." Hearing himself say it out loud, Jackie realized that he actually kind of liked the idea. "And the reason he *wanted* the store was to make enough money to send his kids to college one day. And then from there, I'd lead into why I want to go to college. You know. Heartwarming and shit." Jackie's eyes darted back to the poster. "I mean... and feces."

Flounder blinked. "Who's applying to Cornell? You, or your dad?"

"I mean, *I* am, though I can't say he'd *never* want to try going back to school—"

"Then why are you trying to impress them with how great someone *else* is? What have *you* accomplished? What is *your* purpose?"

Jackie opened his mouth, ready to answer. But as nothing came out, he realized he didn't have anything to say. And he doubted any of Flounder's posters could help him with that.

To continue reading *The Making of a Small-Town Beauty King* head over to Amazon for the paperback or Kindle version.

ACKNOWLEDGMENTS

First and foremost, I'd like to acknowledge Lauri Dietz, who did a fabulous job editing this book. Thank you so much for all of your hard work, especially in such a time crunch. This book would not be what it is today without you.

I also want to give a shout-out to the DePaul University Center for Writing-based Learning, which supported me as a writer so much throughout the process of completing and publishing this book. Special thanks to Sarah Tierney, who helped so much with revisions.

Additionally, thank you to my amazing critique group who discussed this novel with me in its earliest stages. Emily, Nancy, Amy, Rebecca, and Malayna: I greatly appreciate all of your advice and encouragement as I worked my way through my first draft. I also want to recognize Stuart Dybek, who was my professor at Northwestern when I originally wrote this as a short story in 2015, and who encouraged me to expand on it, ultimately resulting in this novel.

Thank you to my parents, Lola and Jeff, who not only have encouraged my career as a writer from the very beginning, but also supported me trying something a little different than the picture books about cute dogs I usually write. And a special shout-out goes to my partner, Tyler, who listens to me complain about how much I hate my boobs all day, but still loves me regardless.

Finally, thank you to the entire city of Chicago for always providing the perfect setting, not only for my novel, but also for my life.

ABOUT THE AUTHOR

SAVY is a Chicago author, journalist, editor, and artist. Before *Sculpt Yourself*, she was best known for her Furever Home Friends children's book series, which introduces kids to new social justice issues through stories of real rescue dogs.

She has worked as a music journalist for *Halftime Magazine* and *Yamaha SupportED* since 2015. She also teaches kids' creative writing workshops at Open Books in Downtown Chicago and provides freelance editing services for other writers.

SAVY graduated from Northwestern University in 2015 and is currently pursuing her Master's in Writing & Publishing at DePaul University.

SAVY also has a young-adult book, *The Making of a Small-Town Beauty King*, currently available on Amazon, and a writing self-help workbook, *The Portable Writer's Confidante,* available for free when you subscribe to her mailing list at savyleiser.com.

You can also visit SAVY on Twitter and Instagram at @savyleiser, and on Facebook at /savyleiserwriter.